WEDDING CAKE MURDER

AN ARIZONA SUMMERS MYSTERY
BOOK ONE

I0545701

SUSAN KEENE

OTHER PUBLICATIONS BY SUSAN KEENE

The Kate Nash Mysteries

Finding Lizzy Smith (Book 1)
Who's Roxy Watkins? (Book 2)
The Untimely Death of Ivy Tucker (Book 3)

Stand Alone
Tattered Wings
The Twisted Mind of Cletus Compton

Publishing Coordinator – Sharon Kizziah-Holmes

Published by Bent Willow Books

ISBN -13: 978-1-945669-99-6

DEDICATION

To everyone who loves dogs,
mystery, and good food.

Acknowledgments

A special thanks to Blenna DeHart , Shirley McCann, Tierney James and Sharon Kizziah-Holmes who are always there for me and Chili and Gambie who keep me company day after day.

Follow your dreams. What have you got to lose?

CHAPTER ONE

As I opened the door to the restaurant I heard my mother's voice echo from the kitchen. She barked orders like a drill sergeant. No telling what she was up to. She never set out to raise havoc, yet catastrophe followed her around like a puppy dog.

To stop her tirade, I walked up, stood behind her, and tapped her lightly on the shoulder. She jumped forward, turned around and put her hand over her heart. "Arizona Summers, you're going to be the death of me yet."

"Mom what's going on? Why are you yelling at the kitchen staff? And in a voice, I might add, that could shatter crystal."

She said nothing but stepped aside so I could enter the belly of the café where the food was prepared. I looked around. "My goodness, James, why's all the bread dough still unbaked? We open in less than an

1

hour."

My mother, who now stood behind me, found her tongue and answered before the chef had a chance to speak. "We were running late. I told the cooks to dispense with the bread and to use the ovens for the desserts."

James looked my way and shrugged his shoulders.

With my hands on my hips I turned to face her. To deal with my mother could be compared to tackling a blizzard without a coat and hat.

I looked at her and stifled a laugh. She wore a teal green tank covered with a long cardigan in pale yellow. From the waist down, she wore only her underwear. Due to the length of her top I doubt the staff noticed.

"Mother, there's an order in which we do things around here. You taught it to me when I was a child and you went over it enough times I repeated it in my sleep.

"We fix the main dishes, sides, salads and the bread. Once those are finished we bake the pies and cakes. People eat dessert last. We have more time to prepare those than the main courses. I know you haven't forgotten so what's up?"

Every day it became clearer why the younger generation took over the cafe when their parent reached her seventy-fifth birthday. I was the fifth generation of Summers to run Moonstone Lake's favorite dining spot.

Some days I wondered if I would survive Emma's interference. In my childhood I called her Emma to catch her attention. Like many busy moms she could block out my constant interruptions.

Sunday brunch took my full attention. I asked her if I could speak to her in the hall. Once we were face to face I said, "I know you like to be in charge but it doesn't work anymore. Please go home and get dressed if you want to mingle with the diners. I suggest you don't do it in your under pants."

She looked down, raised her sweater a little and said, "I'm dressed."

"And you look very nice; from the waist up. I believe skirt or slacks would set off your lovely outfit better than your granny panties."

She turned on her heel and lumbered out the side door. Too many years of restaurant food, mostly desserts, had taken its toll. She looked back to get in the last word. "I don't wear granny panties."

I watched until she disappeared.

Once I heard the door close I returned to the kitchen to try to salvage the day. James walked over to stand beside me. "I'm sorry Ary. I never know what to say to her."

"I know, James, it isn't your fault. I'll call the Amazin' Glazin' and see if they can spare any bread. Meanwhile put as many loaves as possible in the ovens."

The bakery offered us fifteen loaves. I walked across the Boardwalk to pick them up.

Dottie Wittmore had run the Amazin' Glazin' Bakery for as long as I could remember. The aroma of pastries and breads wafted out to the sidewalk. I smelled chocolate, peppermint and fresh rye. I smiled to myself. You'd think the smells would mingle and give off a toxic fume. Somehow they stayed separate. I lingered outside to savor the aroma.

The bakery was full. Both cash registers had lines at least six customers deep. I waved at Dottie and stood to the side, out of the way, until she had time for me.

A young couple sat in the back under an arch in an area decorated like a wedding dome. Many brides and grooms sat there over the years to design their wedding cakes.

Stacy Young and a handsome young man were seated in two of the four chairs arranged around a small heart-shaped table. He had his hand on hers and smiled every time she spoke. What caught my eye were the two women who sat with them. I knew one to be Stacy's mother, Denise. She and I frequented the same book club. The other lady looked out of place in her purple feathered hat, long black coat, brown orthopedic shoes and white gloves.

I watched the four of them. The lady in black threw a hissy-fit. I couldn't hear the conversation but her gestures and tones were unmistakable. I knew the other three and the cake designer had to have been horrified when the bakery became dead silent and the patrons all turned to stare at them.

The woman stood and in a voice the entire shop could hear yelled. "I knew this wedding would be a joke. I should have insisted the ceremony and reception be held in Boston. There's no way this man is a professional cake designer, the church only holds a hundred guests and the reception is at a diner whose claim to fame is a Sunday Brunch."

She looked down at her son. I half expected venom to spurt from her mouth. "And I don't care what your reasoning. I refuse to allow you to have a gray armadillo-shaped groom's cake with gray icing and red cream filling."

As she finished her rude comments I thought of my mother. She had become an instant angel in my mind.

I put my hand over my mouth to stifle a laugh as I visualized the armadillo cake and its gooey filling. On her way out the woman knocked into my skinny frame which caused me to hit the wall behind me. Her feathered hat sailed off her head. No one moved. She reached down picked it up slammed it down cockeyed on her head and stormed toward the door.

She didn't offer an apology. I said an aggravated "Excuse me," as she left. She turned and glared.

Dottie called me to the counter. Fifteen loaves of various varieties of bread stuck out of two huge brown paper bags. "I thought you baked your own bread. Everything all right over there?"

"Yes we lost track of time today." I nodded toward Michael, the cake designer. "What just happened?"

"The groom's mother's a witch. I'm being kind. They've been here three separate times to pick out a cake. The wedding is in less than six weeks. His mother doesn't like anything. I swear, if someone gave her a million dollars she wouldn't take it because it would be the wrong shade of green.

"I told Michael not to put up with it. We don't need business that bad. I wonder how his mother would get along with Suzie, who ices the cakes at Discount Grocery. They're the next closest thing to a bakery within thirty-miles.

"Mike said he hated to send them away. He and

Stacy became close friends when she worked here during her college breaks."

I took the bag she handed me. "Who's the groom? He's a real cutie; he obviously has the patience of a saint if he sat through that with his mother more than once."

"Stacy introduced him as Dillon Freedman. We don't have to guess where he's from; his mother has screamed it enough. Can you imagine comparing our little town of twenty-two hundred to Boston and its hundreds of thousands of people?"

I turned toward the door. "It takes all kinds. I'd better get back. We open in ten minutes. What do I owe you?"

"Oh honey, I'll bill you. You run along."

On the way back I thought about Stacy's mom. The bride's family customarily paid for most of a wedding. Mrs. Young called a few weeks earlier to schedule a time to meet and select the food for the reception. I got a chill at the thought of having to deal with the groom's mother. At least I had seen her in action and knew what to expect.

The kitchen had settled down by the time I got back. James and one of the line cooks sliced the bread I brought with me.

The waiters and waitresses were lined up for the little talk I had with the entire crew as often as I could before we opened. I likened it to the stewardess who stands in the front of the plane to explain to the passengers how to survive a crash. They were there and attentive but I knew if push came to shove we'd all go down with the ship.

They needed a reminder more than ever on brunch

day. "Everyone looks neat and clean, thank you. Remember; keep water glasses, coffee cups, soft drinks and tea glasses full.

"Remove plates from the tables in a timely manner. You don't have to put up with cursing, abuse, touching or general orneriness. Do not handle it yourself. Keep smiling and come get me. I'll take care of it. Mitch and Sara, take section 1, Stan and April 2, Mark and Benny, 3 and Jan and Patty, 4. Good luck out there."

I didn't actually view the dining room as a war zone. We rarely had any problems.

Mom and the bread situation slowed me down. I hadn't changed out of my running clothes. I yelled at my best friend and aunt who stood at the hostess podium. "Sandy, I'll be back in five minutes."

As I went home to change I thought about my Aunt Sandy and how expertly she directed traffic every Sunday. If left unattended and allowed to seat themselves, some customers acted like a herd of cows who tried to get through a narrow gate at the same time. If it were not for my mother's youngest sister, there would be a weekly stampede nearly as dangerous as the Running of the Bulls in Pamplona.

People pushed and shoved to commandeer a seat as close to the buffet table as possible. To some it equated to tickets on the fifty-yard line at a professional football game. A seat near the buffet line became prime real estate on Sundays. The closer people were seated to the food the less time they stood and line in more time they had to eat.

I hated the *all you can eat* concept. Too many diners took it as a challenge. I preferred *all you care to eat.*

CHAPTER TWO

We opened at five thirty every morning for breakfast and closed at nine o'clock each night. We didn't serve anyone after eight p.m. It gave everyone a chance to finish their meal without having to keep the doors open late into the night. Sunday Brunch ran from eleven a.m. until two p.m. We closed the rest of the day.

Customers lined up two hours before we opened on brunch days to guarantee a seat close to the food bar.

Food had never been my motivator, not healthy food anyway. I could eat more junk food than any three kids put together.

We'd been open about an hour. I took a minute to run over to Mother's apartment and make sure she hadn't done anything else to sabotage herself or the day.

I knocked and opened the door without waiting for a reply. "You're late Mom, we've already opened. Several people have asked about you. Don't you think you should go down and mingle?"

"I don't want to get in your way." There were times she sat like a petulant child and glared at me. I wondered if I ever acted the same way; most likely.

Sometimes I didn't know how to approach her. A codicil in my great-great grandmother's will stated clearly, the oldest daughter would take over as manager and owner of the Moonstone Lake Café on her mother's seventy-fifth birthday, that was five years ago. When the elder Summers ladies retired they had a choice to wander around and chat with the customers, travel, take up painting, mountain climbing, deep sea fishing or anything that tickled her fancy. Mother didn't appear to have a fancy.

She didn't hide her dissatisfaction with forced retirement. She chose to step into the daily routine of the restaurant as much as possible. Personally I would have let her work as long as she wanted. My ancestor must have been a wise woman. She knew no business could handle two women of equal status in charge. The younger of the two would never be able to command the authority she needed.

I walked to her chair, knelt, and put my hand on her knee.

She promptly rose, went into her bedroom and slammed the door behind her.

I stared at the closed door but nothing happened. The door couldn't shed any light on my problems with my mother.

I went back to work.

Sandra Summers Jenkins, Emma's youngest sister, had put on a little weight over the past few years. It enhanced her good looks. She smiled at each customer as they came through the door. She greeted the clean, dirty, poor and wealthy all with the same friendly smile. Everybody loved Aunt Sandra.

I went over and helped her seat people. I looked to see who was next and there stood the wedding party. Jackson Young, Stacy's father stepped forward. "We need a table for six."

"Hum. Six." Sandy mumbled to herself as she scoured the seating chart to find a suitable table.

I stood next to Stacy. When Sandy told me the table number I smiled and said, "Table for six, right this way."

The woman I'd observed at the bakery wore a bright pink pill box hat with a coat and gloves of a lighter shade. I looked down to see if her orthopedic shoes came in colors. They did not.

She walked up to me and stood so close I had to take a step backward so as not to lose my balance. "How perceptive of you dear to realize there are six of us." Mrs. Freedman hadn't learned any manners since I saw her at the bakery.

Stacy smiled at me. "Ruth," she patted the woman on the wrist. "This is Arizona Summers. She's the owner of this restaurant."

The woman looked around and raised her chin. "I'm sorry for you Miss Summers."

I kept the smile on my face but secretly I hoped she'd trip and fall on her nose. I walked them to the last table in the main dining room as far from the food as I could. If Mrs. Freedman flew off the handle maybe the debris wouldn't hit anyone.

Dillon stopped me from leaving. "Miss Summers, Stacy has told me all about you and the wonderful food you serve here. I'm so pleased to meet you. This is my dad, Roger Freedman."

I reached out to shake his hand. He smiled and flashed a set of perfect pearly white teeth. The witch ignored me. It was probably for the best.

As I turned to leave the table Mrs. Freedman perked up. "Miss, bring me a menu and coffee; black please."

The way she said it, I got the impression her goal was to try to make me feel small and subservient, neither of which I did easily. "We don't have a menu on Sunday. The coffee is on the beverage bar. Sunday is a buffet. I'm sure you'll find our offerings to your liking. We have sixty items on our brunch bars and your choice of fifteen desserts on the right."

I thought I heard a *harrumph*. "You mean if I want to eat I must get in a line like a pauper in a soup kitchen and fetch my own food? You want me to touch the utensils after all those people and their dirty hands? How gauche."

CHAPTER THREE

Jake Anderson, a diner at the next table, stood and faced Mrs. Freedman. I didn't try to stop him. "Listen lady, if you think you're too good to eat with us common folk, and that you have a right to talk to this fine lady like that; I hope you starve." He had his say and sat down.

I smiled at everyone concerned and headed back to my job.

Later I noticed everyone at the table except Mrs. Freedman had gone to the bar and filled their plates.

Aunt Sandra moved from the hostess station to the cashier booth on the other side of the room. We had it set up with a series of slack ropes much like the ones used in amusement parks to keep people in line.

We closed the entry door at two. No one could exit without going past the cash register.

Aunt Sandy had not interacted with Mrs.

Freedman and I hadn't had time to warn her. When they were ready to check out I stood back to watch.

Sandra took the ticket from Mr. Freedman. "Six adult buffets at $21.95 comes to $131.70.

He handed her a credit card.

Mrs. Freedman, who had been at the end of their group, deep in conversation with Mrs. Young, elbowed her way up to her husband. "You can take one of those dinners off. I didn't eat any of that food."

"I'm sorry ma'am. What didn't you like about our food?"

"I don't like the idea of it. I didn't eat anything and I'll not pay."

Sandra looked up at her and in a soft voice explained. "Whether you ate or not you took up a seat leaving a paying customer with no place to sit."

She glanced back to the woman's husband. While his wife fussed, Sandy ran his card and handed it back to him along with the receipt to sign.

Mrs. Freedman's voice got louder. "This is an outrage. I'll never step foot in this establishment again. I have a mind to call the police."

To stop the situation from escalating, I stepped up. "There's no need for that ma'am."

The groom's mother smiled. She thought she had the upper hand.

I continued and hoped she didn't call my bluff. I had no idea where the police were. "Chief Wesley of the Moonstone Lake police is here. I'll get him for you."

Her husband leaned forward. "That won't be necessary. I apologize for my wife."

She was too busy with her son to hear her husband's comment.

Dillon had leaned over and spoke in his mother's ear. He must have informed her where the reception would be held.

She took a Kleenex from her purse and wiped her brow. "Lord knows I'll never survive this podunk town and redneck wedding." She stomped out; the rest of the party trailed behind her.

Aunt Sandy didn't comment. She looked up, smiled at the next group in line and ignored what had happened a moment earlier.

I loved my Aunt Sandy.

The day arrived for the Young-Freedman wedding party to choose their food. I usually loved to help couples plan for their receptions. My enthusiasm waned at the prospect of another encounter with Mrs. Freedman.

When they arrived Stacey, her Mom and Dillon were alone. "Should we wait for your mother, Dillon?" Is she under the weather?" Secretly I hoped she had dysentery or the Black Plague."

"She's fine. She flew back to Boston to finish some work at the Foundation. She'll be back for the wedding."

I hoped I sounded sincere and not relieved when I said. "That's too bad. Let's go on with your choices for the reception. We have samples of all your selections."

We moved to one of the larger tables. I sat across from the three of them.

The party added and discarded food and kibitzed for nearly two hours.

The final selections were; bacon wrapped button mushrooms in brown butter as the appetizer and baked chicken breast crusted with breadcrumbs, Parmesan cheese, basil and pepper as the main dish. They chose the home-style green beans as the vegetable. Fresh cut garden salads and yeast rolls would be on each table when the guests arrived.. They promised a final guest count two weeks before the ceremony.

I went over the order with them one final time and walked them to the door.

CHAPTER FOUR

I don't know what possessed me to take a different route on my morning jog. It was as though an invisible force pushed me to the lower trail. I'd run the upper path on a daily basis for years. Its red bouncy rubber tarmac surface kept my feet and ankles pain free.

The lower trail needed work. Some parts were smooth and flat, others were bumpy with huge boulders at the edge. Rather than the cushy rubber, the city had covered the lower one with pea gravel. It detoured around pilings and required total concentration to maneuver unscathed.

Most people ran to lose weight. I ran to gain some bulk. Two girls at my lunch table in the fourth grade were on a diet. Both of them were cute and had curves. I remember I wanted curves. I overheard their conversation and learned muscle weighed more than fat. I had run every day since except on the rare occasion the weather wouldn't cooperate. On those days I lifted weights in my apartment. My legs were as solid as concrete. The muscle had done the trick.

As everyone I knew aged they gained weight, not me. I was not just thin when I was a kid but I was skinny enough to hide behind a telephone pole.

In grade school and high school kids teased me until I cried. I had bright red hair to top off my straight up and down torso. The other kids called me Matchstick. They drew pictures of matchsticks and labeled them Arizona. By the time I made it to the sixth grade my shoes were size eleven. Thank goodness no one thought to call me a Pez Dispenser.

The lake's surface had fascinated me since childhood. On days it was crystal clear I stood and stared at it. I'd lived at Moonstone Lake since the age of five. My fascination with it never waned.

I didn't like the lower path yet something compelled me to be there. I cleared my mind and tried to think good thoughts.

It didn't work. Memories of my childhood took over my brain. Half way around the lake I tripped over something and landed on both hands and knees.

My mother told me thousands of times to leave the past in the past. Had I listened chances were pretty good I would not have been on the ground with a raspberry on each knee like a six-year-old.

I turned over and surveyed the extent of my wounds. An object in the water caught my eye. It floated and bobbed up and down with the wake. I stood to take a better look. The longer I stared at it the more details I picked out.

As I looked at the object the more certain I became it was a body. Surely it wasn't. The mesmerizing roll of the water made it look as if it drifted toward the shore.

I stood frozen and picked a point of reference. It took only a minute for me to determine it hadn't moved. We'd had three murders in Moonstone Lake in the last ten years.

My otherwise strong as a tree-limb legs did not want to hold me up. I leaned over and placed a hand over each knee cap and pushed back hard determined not to let them fail me. The sores throbbed under my palms and added to the queasiness of my stomach and my shaking body. I sat on the ground.

I yelled and screamed for someone to come. I called until my voice gave out and became no louder than a whisper.

Harry Cotton came into sight and ran toward me. He didn't exactly run. The girth around his belly swayed from one side to the other with every step like a balloon filled with water. The mere weight of the movement propelled him forward.

I'd suggested a million times he would be best served if he walked. Harry never listened.

He had a phone and dialed 911.

CHAPTER FIVE

The Moonstone Lake Police were the first to arrive. They didn't do anything. Chief Keith Wesley looked through a pair of binoculars and declared the floater a body. He made two phone calls before he came over to me. He took a note pad out of his pocket and began to interrogate me. "What's your name?"

"Arizona Summers."

He looked down at me for the first time. "You're Arizona Summers?" He reached down to help me up. Once I stood he looked me up and down. "From your reputation I expected more."

I moved my hands from my sides and rested them on my hips. "Well now, you're a real charmer aren't you?"

He ignored me but I was certain he'd heard what I said.

"Tell me what you saw and when, Miss

Summers." He said my name as if it put a bad taste in his mouth.

"I was on my morning jog. I tripped and fell and when I began to get up I saw the body."

He tapped the pen on his tablet. "That's pretty succinct. Is that all you remember?"

"That's all there is to it."

His square jaw twitched. I knew Moonstone Lake had hired a new police chief but no one had told me about his striking good looks.

I could describe him in two words—my type. His military style haircut set off a chiseled jaw line and his deep brown eyes were difficult to ignore. His low slow southern drawl sounded totally out of place in the Ozarks. The difference between a boot heel accent and one from the Deep South could be likened to the difference between rock'n roll and opera.

Geez, how could I have let my mind linger on such trivial details when some poor person floated dead in the lake? "I remember every moment of my jog this morning. The thing is— none of it has anything to do with the body out there."

He put the pen to the paper once more. "Let me be the judge of that."

No way would I tell him an invisible force made me choose the lower lake path. "The water looked so pristine this morning I decided to run down here where I could get a better view."

He pointed to the high path. "So you couldn't enjoy the lake from up there?"

I turned on my heel to walk away from him. "I'm leaving."

He put his hand on my arm. "Hey Randy get the

lady a blanket. She's freezing down here."

I wanted to leave so I played his game and expanded my answer. "When I turned toward the lake I saw something floating. I realized it was a person. I couldn't call 911 because I don't carry a phone when I run."

He glared down at me with such a hard look I had to focus not to cower. He stood well over six feet tall. "Miss Summers, do you know how dangerous it is to be outside away from everything and everyone with no means of communication?"

At that point I was sure my face matched my hair. I hadn't been chastised like that since I traded my third grade teacher's hardboiled egg with a real one and she cracked it on her desk. "Yes sir, I've learned my lesson. Next time I spy a body in the lake I'll have a phone to call it in."

Harry stepped up. "I called. I carry my phone, wallet and my car keys."

Wesley gave him a look I couldn't read and walked closer to the shore. A Coast Guard boat was now docked next to the body.

CHAPTER SIX

We looked on silently. I had no idea what the others thought but I wanted to cry. Someone died.

It seemed like hours before they grabbed the body with a grappling hook and dragged it onto the deck of the Coast Guard cutter.

I heard the Chief's radio squawk. I sneaked up behind him to try to listen to the conversation. "Chief, Captain Donavan, Missouri Coast Guard, we retrieved the body from the lake. The clothes suggest it is a woman. We can't tell for sure but I think she's been in there awhile."

"Thanks Donavan. Please transport her to the public access at Marshall Cove. I'll have the proper paper work and personnel to take her off your hands. It might take me an hour or so."

Before the boat captain signed off he said, "one more question. Do you have any missing person's reports?"

Wesley answered. "We have one; a Ruth Freedman reported missing a few days ago."

I had taken another step closer to Keith Wesley. He turned around and we stood nose to nose. Nose to muscular chest described it better. "You can go now Miss Summers. If we need anything else we'll contact you." I offered my address. "Arizona, everyone knows where you live."

Mrs. Freedman-dead. How horrible. Did she fall off a dock, out of a boat or fall in the lake while on a walk? Did someone murder her? And lastly I realized it might not have been Mrs. Freedman.

In Sandra's free time I knew she'd be home with her nose in a book. If not there she roamed around The Plot Thickens Book Store across the street.

Two generations ago one of my ancestors bought a four-plex. It sat so close to the restaurant none of us had to leave the building to go home or to work. It sat between Moonstone Lake Café and a bed and breakfast.

Mom lived downstairs on the left, James, one of the chefs, on the right. Sandra and I lived upstairs, she on the right and me on the left.

Often I remembered the old saying, familiarity breeds contempt.

I knocked on Aunt Sandy's door. She answered immediately. "Ary, there you are. I was worried. There have been more sirens in the last two hours than I've heard in the last two years. What happened?"

Without being invited I plopped down on the couch. "Remember the grouchy old lady who didn't

THE WEDDING CAKE MYSTERY

want to pay for her dinner Sunday? I found her dead in the lake."

Sandy looked at me. Her cats, Wynken, Blynken and Nod were curled together at the other end. I sat down so hard they bounced. "What happened to your knees?"

I looked down. Sand and rocks were stuck in the tears in my tights. "I tripped over a rock and fell. As I got up, I saw her body. It was awful."

She left the room and returned with a dish of warm water, a cloth, peroxide and a pair of scissors. Before she did anything she cut my pants off above the knee. They were toast anyway. She sat the bowl on the table next to me. "Let's clean that so it doesn't get infected."

I looked out the window lost in thought. What if it wasn't an accident? I didn't want to speculate. Somewhere someone cared about that horrible woman, her husband, her son and maybe countless others. And the wedding; the church had been reserved, our café', the wedding cake and the flowers. What a mess it could turn out to be. I tried to pull my mind back to my legs. After all, it could have been someone else not the old bag herself. Her husband said she flew back to Boston. Somehow she would have had to have gotten to the airport.

My injury looked like nothing once the dirt and grime were gone. "I don't know what possessed me to change my routine. I started out as I do every morning. I'm not sure what happened but I had the strongest pull I've ever had. I was compelled to run the lower path. Mom always told me *Prayer is you talking to God; intuition is God talking to you.* Don't laugh, but maybe I was supposed to find the body."

Sandra picked up Nod and moved the other two over so she could sit next to me. "I wouldn't laugh at you. I guess glamour boy was there."

I wished my face hadn't betrayed me. I knew it turned crimson again. "Yes, first one on the scene. His attitude toward me could freeze the desert. I had no idea he was so handsome. Unfortunately it didn't make up for his nasty disposition. No one around us had to guess how he feels about me. He doesn't like me and he doesn't hide it. He's no Chief Chase."

She reached over and patted my shoulder. "How do you know? Maybe he was stressed about the drowning. It'll be his first big case since he arrived."

I stood so I could see further down the lake. Police cars were still there. A couple of dozen onlookers had assembled with more on the way. "Maybe he doesn't like women."

She shook her head no. "Maybe he's as shy as you are. I suggest you stop jogging and working out. You have great muscle tone but you need to gain some weight."

"I doubt if my looks have anything to do with why he doesn't like me. Before Chief Chase left he told me he intended to pave the way for me to help Keith Wesley just the way I helped him. Obviously the idea didn't thrill him."

I rose to leave which meant I had to untangle myself from one of the cats. "If I don't go to the gym, run and bike ride I would spend all of my time at the café. How am I going to meet anyone there?"

She stood and came over next to me. "My sweet girl, the best way to find someone is to stop looking.

When you least expect it the right person will come along. Besides, muscles or no muscles, for some reason all of your workouts don't get rid of that little paunch you've had all your life. When you turn sideways you look like a snake that swallowed an egg." Sandra began to laugh. She laughed until she nearly fell to the floor.

I took it in the vain it was meant and laughed with her. The snake comment was something my Mom had said to me a thousand times. I didn't usually find it humorous; or true. For once I laughed at myself.

When the morning paper came I combed through it for information on the identity of the body in the water. I found no mention of a drowning.

A majority of Moonstone Lake Boardwalk residents already knew about it. We were a small community on the south side of the lake. Of the twenty-two hundred people in the town, we claimed a little over four hundred. Most of the crime and mayhem happened on the north side. The population on the other side was five times our little section. We were like two different towns. Their advantage came because they had more restaurants, a movie theater and more name brand stores, which included a Discount Grocery, Johnny's Steak House and the big Sunshine Hotel and Water Park. The police station was on our side. I found it strange it wasn't built next to the courthouse on the square on the north side.

Our side had quaint shops, unique stores, finery, eateries and entertainment. Officially our side of town was known as The Boardwalk, and was recognized Nationwide.

CHAPTER SEVEN

Three days had passed since I saw the body in the lake. The paper said they were waiting for a positive identification. On the third day the authorities used the excuse they had not notified the next of kin.

The fourth day the headline read. BODY OF WEALTHY BOSTON SOCIALITE FOUND IN MOONSTONE LAKE.

It went on to tell about the wedding of a local girl, Stacy Young.

At the end it stated the cause of death as unknown. Maybe she hadn't drowned?

I went back to my routine. I jogged on the trail, went to work, read and had an occasional glass of wine with Sandra. The entire time I carried my phone.

On one particularly beautiful spring day someone ran behind me. The hair stood up on the back of my neck. My entire body grew hot. When I slowed down, he did and when I sped up. so did whoever shadowed me. I picked up my pace, took my phone out of my pocket, dialed 911, but didn't hit the send button.

I stopped and spun around. Behind me there stood a skinny, scrawny. bony, dog. It had long curly matted hair the color of nutmeg.

"Where did you come from?"

The dog took a few steps backward and sat. It raised a paw in the air for a handshake. I walked back and took hold of it.

"Are you a boy or a girl?"

The dog stood, walked in a circle and sat down again. "A girl." I said out loud. "You look like you've been on your own for a while. Are you thirsty?"

I answered my own question. "Of course you're not. You're on the edge of a five thousand acre lake. You do look hungry. Want to go home with me? I'll get you something to eat and we'll try to find your owner."

The dog was either brilliant or it was a fluke. She wagged her tail when I asked if she wanted to go home with me. She whined when I mentioned finding her home.

On any other day I would have run another two miles. On this day I turned around and started toward home. The poor dog didn't look as if it could last much longer without food.

I knocked on the back door of the kitchen. James opened it. "Could you find something for this dog to eat? I believe she's starving."

"Sure Ary. But I wouldn't feed her too much at once. It might make her sick. Looks like days since she's had any food."

I sat on the back stoop with the dog until James showed up with a bowl. He handed it to me. "What's that?"

"Its rice and ground beef. It'll help her get stronger. I made enough for a few days."

"I don't intend to keep the dog."

"Ary, you're fooling yourself. That dog isn't going anywhere. You might as well bathe her, take her to the vet to get her shots, see if she's fixed and give her a name."

While we talked, the dog inhaled the food.

I walked around to the front entrance of the apartments, the dog followed. I went in and closed the door. After a few minutes I opened it to see if she was gone but she lay asleep on the stoop in the sun.

Jeez, I didn't want a dog yet I opened the door. "Come on, might as well clean you up." She walked in and without hesitation walked up to the second floor and stood in front of my apartment door.

I had the last thing I wanted— a dog.

My cell phone rang. I looked at the caller ID, Moonstone Lake Police Department flashed on the screen. Sure I'll be down in the morning. Is ten okay?"

Sergeant Randy Malone had called to say he wanted to relay a message from Chief Wesley. *The Chief has more questions to ask you. He needs to clear up a few details.* Why did they want me? I told them all I knew about the body. Could I be a suspect?

I tried to put it out of my mind. Me as a suspect

was a ridiculous thought.

The dog looked and smelled much better after her bath. I ran downstairs and picked up the rest of the food from James.

I gave her more food and sat on the couch to watch her. She had the size of a Labrador, the hair of a Sheepdog and the coloring of a Bloodhound. The name, Nutmeg, suited her to a tea.

She went to the restaurant with me but I knew she couldn't be around the food. I introduced her to Sandy and asked if she could lay down in the front foyer with her.

Nutmeg didn't wait for an answer. She trotted over to the hostess podium and scampered under it out of the way.

All evening my mind wandered back to the call from Randy. Why did Wesley want to see me? I told him what little I knew: twice.

After the last diner left I asked Sandra if she had time to talk. "Yes." she looked down at the dog. "I know you've never wanted a pet so what's that."

"She's a different kind of dog. Remember the *horse of different color*? This is a dog of another type. She seems more human than dog." I looked at Nutmeg who sat at my feet and wagged her tail.

Sandy reached over and petted her on the head. "But she's still a dog and the cats don't like dogs."

"Let's try it once. If she doesn't like the cats or gets aggressive I'll take her home."

Sandy looked apprehensive but nodded okay.

Once we had a glass of wine. I told her my concerns. "The chief wants me to come in tomorrow morning. What if Ruth Freedman was murdered? Do you think I'm a suspect?"

"I doubt it but you did find the body. Sometimes if the police ask the right questions a witness remembers a fact or a person they didn't realize they saw or knew."

"Sandy, you've been reading too many mysteries again."

Mom was born when her mother was sixteen. Aunt Sandra didn't come along until thirty years later. She called herself a change of life baby.

They were more like Mother and Daughter than sisters. Mom would soon be eighty-one and Sandy turned fifty less than a month before.

She sipped her wine. "You had an altercation with the deceased at brunch. For that matter, I had one with her at the cashier's table the same night. I wonder if they'll call me in."

She got up and went to the kitchen and came back with a pen and paper.

I pointed to Nutmeg. "Look at that." Wynken, Blynken and Nod were curled up with her on the floor. She lie on her side and let them snuggle with her for a nap.

We moved to the kitchen table so Sandy could write. "Okay," she said, "let's make a suspect list."

"I can think of several people who had altercations with the old bag and I only saw her twice. On her third trip to the bakery she insulted Michael Ames. She told him he wasn't a cake designer. She actually called him a redneck at the top of her lungs. I stood next to Dottie during the exchange. She had certainly had enough.

"Stacy and Dillon had been to the bakery with his

mother on three separate occasions to pick out a cake. She stormed out alone; hopefully they picked the one they wanted after she left.

"I didn't see her again until they came to the buffet on Sunday. She fussed at me over the entire concept of food bars. Jake Anderson had his say when she was impolite to me. Then there is you, Sandy. You made her pay for a meal she refused to eat."

Sandy went down the names on her notepad. "My, we have quite a list here, me, you, Jake Anderson, Michael Ames, Dottie Wittmore, Stacy, Dillon and Stacy's parents, Denise and Jackson."

I stood, walked back to the living room and sat on the floor with Nutmeg and the cats. "Ten people and I only saw her twice. I know she visited the florist and the church. If we want to dig deeper I bet she had a comment or two about Mable Hayes at the church and her ability to play organ music."

Sandy looked down at me. "I have a problem with Mable's musical ability myself."

She retrieved the glasses from the coffee table and held them in the air. "More wine?"

I shook my head no. "I'll have water. We left out Ruth's husband, Roger. I don't know how long they were married, but I know a little of her goes a long way. Every time I see him he's soft spoken and polite. Could be he held it in so long, he exploded."

I moved to a chair to drink my water. Nutmeg shook the cats off and came over to sit next to me. "Ten suspects including us, if you discount us, which I intend to do, there are eight. "

She scooted her chair back to allow Blynken to

jump on her lap. "Who do you think the murderer is?"

I stroked Nutmeg. "I vote for Mr. Freedman, or Dillon."

Sandra leaned forward to put her elbows on the table and rested her chin in her hands "Why not the cake designer?"

"He and Stacy are good friends. I think his reaction would be disgust, but I doubt he's violent. I've known him forever. When he isn't working on cakes, he paints. He did the horse mural on the wall at the movies on Spruce Street."

"I didn't know that."

"You need to branch out and move past the book store, café and book club."

"Thanks, I'll take it under advisement. As a matter of fact, I am thinking about buying a scooter. They are small and inexpensive and I won't need a license to ride it. I could explore the north side. I love movies and they have the theater."

Nutmeg growled, went to the door and sat. Sandy followed her. "Do you think someone's out there?"

"I doubt it. I was the last one in and I locked the main door. You and I haven't gone out and Mother is probably resting. James is with the cleaning crew down in the kitchen."

The dog scratched the door. Sandy said, "Don't tell me the dog is housetrained too."

"Sure she is. I told you she's more human than dog. She knows what's going on long before I do. Yesterday she brought me my cell phone before it rang. How can that be?"

Sandy stood and walked over to us. The cats had

scrambled out of the room, another sign things were not as they should have been. I slowly opened the door. Nutmeg ran down the steps and sat in front of Mother's door.

The door stood ajar and every light in the place was on. The living room TV echoed off the walls. I searched every room, Mother wasn't there.

"Should we call 911?" Sandy asked.

Nutmeg barked and danced until we followed her. She led us to the restaurant kitchen. There sat mom eating cookies. The counters still smelled like cleaning solution.

My aunt pulled a stool up next to her. "Emma, what are you doing?"

The look Mother gave her was one I couldn't read. "Sandra, have you lost your eyesight? I'm eating cookies."

Sandra put her hand on top of her sister's. "Do you realize how late it is? You should be in bed."

"Why is that Sandra? Because I have so many appointments and I might be late for one because I didn't get enough sleep?"

I had not said a word. She turned to me and asked. "So Arizona, do I have a bedtime now?" She looked at the dog. "What's that and why is it in *my* kitchen?"

I became defensive. "Oh, that's Nutmeg, she lives with me, and it is *our* kitchen."

Mother stood. When she did, the entire tray of cookies fell to the floor.

Sandra bent down to pick them up.

Mother looked at the mess on the floor; she laughed and said, "That's the way the cookie crumbles." She walked to the door, turned around, lifted her arm and wiggled her fingers at us before she left.

Nutmeg didn't try to eat the cookies. Sandra fetched the dustpan, I grabbed the broom and we cleaned up the mess. I had no idea why Mother tried so hard to mess up things. She had enough money to go anywhere she wanted or do anything she cared to do.

Sandy picked up the dustpan and waved it at me. "Why does she do that?"

I leaned on the broom. "I refuse to believe she goes on these escapades on purpose."

"It's scary if she doesn't know what she's doing."

"No kidding. I know it's not dementia. She's as sharp as a tack. I think she wanted a cookie and knew where to find one."

CHAPTER EIGHT

I went on my morning run with Nutmeg by my side. It was as though I'd had her forever.

At nine-thirty I walked toward the Police Station. It sat on the west end of the lake with the jail attached to its north end and a large parking lot on the south.

Patrolman Randy Malone manned the desk. We'd gone to high school together. Other than the times he dined at the restaurant, I'd lost track of his life.

He'd asked me out several times in our school days. I accepted twice, the Junior Prom and the Senior Prom. Randy had always been a gentleman. I didn't consider high school as my finest years.

He grinned at me. His eyes disappeared when he grinned. I always wondered how he could smile and see at the same time.

In school he played tight end on the football team and second base on the baseball team. From the looks of him he had remained active. The short sleeves of his uniform were stretched to the limit. He looked more like a wrestler than a police officer. He had gotten better looking with age. "Hi, Ary, haven't seen you in a coon's age. How are you? I go to the café, but you're either off duty or too busy to visit."

"Good to see you, Randy. You must come at the wrong times. I feel like I live there. You can always catch me at Sunday Brunch. I'm there every week."

Geez. Why did I tell him all of that? I sounded desperate for friends and company.

My thoughts were interrupted when Chief Wesley stepped into the room. He didn't have Randy's muscles, but I pictured his chest as hard and strong. His uniform pants clung to powerful legs. It was almost enough to make me forget how rude he had been to me—almost. "Arizona, could you come into my office."

I turned to follow him. I waved at Randy on my way out.

The Chief pointed to a chair on one side of the desk and he took his seat behind it. "Ms. Summers, I need to ask you a few questions. I'll be video and audio recording this little chat. Do you understand your rights or would you like me to Mirandize you?"

"I understand them, but you have to read them to me if you plan to arrest me or charge me with something. I don't know what it could be."

"Are you an attorney now? I thought you were a waitress."

"I'm not a waitress. I am a business owner. Do you plan to charge me with a crime because I work in a restaurant?"

"No, Arizona but this investigation has just begun. Until I know who killed Mrs. Freedman I'm not ruling anyone out."

I sat on the edge of my chair and rested my forearm on his highly polished mahogany desk. "If she drowned, why do you believe someone murdered her?"

"There was no water in her lungs. Try to remember I'm questioning you, you're not questioning me. How is it you happened to be in just the right place to find Ruth Freedman's body?"

I leaned back in my chair with enough force to move it an inch or two away from the desk. "I have told you all of this. Are you hoping I'll make a mistake and you can charge me with her death?"

"Miss Summers, just answer the questions. I'm trying to make a timeline and investigate every moment from when the body was found until now."

I didn't want to smile, but I couldn't help myself. "Don't you think it would be more productive to dig into what happened from the time she left the Young's house until I saw her body in the lake?"

Woo Wee; never in my life had I seen someone's face turn so red so fast. I expected to see steam come out of his ears. "This is the last time I'm going to warn you Ms. Summers. Answer the questions."

I wanted so badly to say, *or you'll lock me up*, but I didn't want to push my luck. "Okay, ask away."

"Why did you run the bottom loop instead of the top like you always do?"

"How do you know I always run the top?"

He took in a big breath and let it out in what could be labeled as nothing but exasperation. "Because you told me the first time I met you."

"I guess I'll tell you again since you forgot or didn't write it down."

"Okay, that's enough, we aren't getting anywhere. So here are the rules. I've heard stories about the cases you helped solve with the last chief. It will not happen with me. Do you understand? Stay out of police business."

"But, Chief, had I not stepped in on the Slack murder, the drifter would have left town and never been brought to justice. In the Carr case, the police didn't even look at Sammy Meek as a suspect. Had I not found the drawings of the bombs, Mr. Meek would be sailing around the world on Mike Carr's money."

I watched his face turn a darker and darker shade of red as I talked.

I didn't care. I intended to have my say. His good looks, sexy smile, charming drawl and black eyes didn't give him any right to talk down to me.

"I didn't snoop or over-step to solve those cases. Chief Paul Chase came to the café on several occasions to talk to me about problems he had with his current case. It wasn't my fault I could put two and two together and get four."

CHAPTER NINE

My powers of observation were honed when I was a child. I stood back and watched everything. I didn't know my parents, the people in the orphanage or, Emma, my new mother. My life hadn't been one to build trust in a child and it stuck with me. It took me years to feel secure in my home and with myself. I became the master at seeing clues others passed up. Nothing was out of place at my home that I didn't notice. Mom and Aunt Sandy came to me to find any lost item. Nine times out of ten, I had seen where they'd put the object they considered lost.

The end result made me a great detective.

He didn't intend to let me go until he finished the speech he had obviously rehearsed. "Arizona Summers. I am not the old chief. I will not tolerate your interference. I will have you arrested for obstruction of justice." He shoved his chair back with a hard push and stood. "You're free to go."

I decided it best to remain quiet. I gave him my nastiest stare and left.

His holier than thou attitude only made me more determined to find Ruth Freedman's killer.

Nutmeg sat in front of the police station door and waited for me. "There's my buddy, ready to go home?"

We moseyed down The Boardwalk, looked in store windows, and waved at friends. Those who weren't busy came out to meet Nutmeg. Most kept dog treats on hand. If she ate many more, she'd have to roll the rest of the way home.

I could see Sandra inside the Plot Thickens. She noticed me and her eyes widened. I went inside. "What happened? Did he tell you why he called you down there?"

I looked around. Three other customers roamed through the aisles and thumbed through books. "Let's go down to the Hug-a-Mug and I'll tell you all about it."

The aroma of coffee floated through the air. Even people who don't like the taste of coffee love the smell. I picked an outside table away from other patrons so Nutmeg wouldn't be in the way. Through the window I saw Tamera and Tiffney, the owners, had a house full. I went inside to place an order. Once we were settled I told Sandra about the warning the new police chief gave me. I also told her my plan. "The police, fire men, ambulance drivers, and the rest of the emergency staff in this town all eat breakfast at our place at one time or another. I'm going to wander around more and see what I can find out."

Sandy took a sip of her coffee. "What about your friend at the newspaper, Liz Austin? You two used to be tight. What happened?"

"She started going with that scuzz-crud, Mick Dudley. He didn't want her to have any friends."

"Ary, you shouldn't call people names. Apparently, Liz likes him,"

I didn't answer right away. I stopped to take care of the dog. I carried a small backpack in which I had a collapsible bowl, a bottle of water, napkins and small plastic bags for Nutmeg. Once I took care of her, I answered. "He didn't want her to have friends. He wanted complete control over her. The abuse he raged on her lasted for over a year. One of her friends at the paper guessed what was going on and turned him in."

Sandy nodded yes when Tiffney came by and asked if we wanted more coffee. "What happened?"

"She pressed charges and he's in jail, but not for beating Liz. He had a gang and together they stole cars and sold them to a chop-shop."

"Nice guy! You didn't answer why you two aren't close anymore. Do you want something to eat?"

I reached down to pet Nutmeg. "I don't want anything. James and Lewis have perfected some new dishes for the buffet. If I eat now, I won't want to taste them when I get back but I have too.

"Where Liz is concerned, maybe she was embarrassed. I tried for a month or so to bring her out of her shell. You know how it is at the restaurant. It can be all-consuming if you let it. Now as I think about it, she and I had so much fun. I'll call her.

Better yet, I'll stop by the paper."

We said our goodbyes. Sandy headed back to the book store. I walked in the other direction toward Liz's office.

CHAPTER TEN

The Moonstone Reflection, our daily newspaper, sat at the end of The Boardwalk on the side farthest from the lake. I had to pass Penguin's Frozen Treats on my way. It was one of the few times I didn't stop in for an ice cream. Dreamsicles were my favorite.

Liz had always aspired to be a newspaper reporter. In high school she was editor of the paper. She helped put out the yearbook four years in a row.

I opened the door like I owned the place and let the dog follow me in. Liz's desk had always been on the second floor. The building sat high enough for me to see the lake from her station.

There sat Liz, earphones in, fully engrossed in her task. Her curly blond hair hung in ringlets around her face. When I saw her again, I remembered how tiny she was. Mick could have killed her with two well-placed punches. I waved my hand in front of her.

"Liz got a minute."

She stood, grinned, and ran around the desk to hug me. "I'm so glad to see you. I've wanted to call or come by so many times, but I couldn't get over my fear of how dumb you probably thought I was."

She pulled out a chair and invited me to sit. She spotted the dog. "Who's this beautiful creature?"

As if on cue, Nutmeg walked over to her, sat down, and raised her paw to shake hands.

"My goodness, Ary, I didn't know you could train dogs."

The dog walked back to me and sat near my left leg. "I didn't train her, I found her. It's a story for another time."

Her cell phone rang. She held up one finger in a wait a minute signal. I couldn't help but listen to her side of the call. "Wait, I don't want to get this wrong. Mrs. Freedman didn't drown. She had a foreign substance in her system. You don't want me to write about it because you want to use it to try and trap the killer. No water in her lungs, she'd been in the water for about three days.

"Certainly, I can write anything you want if it will help catch the person who murdered her. Okay, Chief Wesley, will Do." She laid her cell phone on her desk and said "Sorry about that. The Freedman murder has everyone spooked."

I had to ask. "Do you know who they think did it?"

"Sorry, Ary, I don't know, and what little I do know is sworn to secrecy."

"I understand. I know you have a big story, but do you have time for lunch or dinner?"

"Of course I do. Let me look at the big board." Nutmeg and I followed her. She stood on her tip toes, found her initials among all the others and ran her finger down to the date. "Looks like after today I'm off every evening, barring a major event call."

"How about tomorrow night? We're busy until about six-thirty and then Sandra can handle it."

"I'm so excited you came by. I'll be there tomorrow evening." We hugged again.

CHAPTER ELEVEN

James and Lewis, our number one chef, waited for me in the kitchen. Each had several plates of food in front of him for me to sample. Lewis had been with the restaurant for over fifteen years. James had been there a little over a year. Either one of them had the skill to move on to a bigger place with better pay. They stayed with us and we were blessed.

The two grabbed stools and sat across the counter from me. "Do you have a dish to replace the asparagus bacon quiche?" I asked.

James pushed a casserole dish in front of me. I took a small bite and then a larger one. "Oh, my goodness, what's in this? The smell is intoxicating. The chicken is tender and the cheese melts in your mouth, I love the seasoning."

He beamed. Everyone loves a compliment. "It's rich. I started with broiled shredded chicken, three varieties of cheese, sour cream, chicken broth, onions, garlic, salt and pepper. I gather, from your reaction, you like it."

"Heaven's yes, you can't tell? Did you cost it out?"

He pushed the note with his calculations over to me. "I certainly did."

I took another bite. "I say we lose the asparagus dish. If I didn't need to leave room for the rest of this lovely food," I raised my arm and swept it above the row of dishes. "I could eat the entire pan. What do you have Lewis?"

Lewis had to be the best pastry chef in all of Missouri.

"I want to stop serving pumpkin pie unless it is Christmas or Thanksgiving. I can tell by the leftovers people are tired of it. The servers and busboys don't even want to take it home.

"I have popcorn balls for the children and peanut butter balls for the adults, although we won't specify who gets what. I can make twelve dozen peanut butter balls for the cost of one pumpkin pie, and popcorn balls cost next to nothing. They were hard to figure. I'd say three cents apiece."

While Lewis talked, I tasted the peanut butter and chocolate dessert. "My goodness, they melt in your mouth. Is that honey you used to hold them together?"

He shook his finger at me. "Ary, you know I must have a few secrets."

"I would have never thought to put popcorn balls on the buffet."

We went over the other dishes. They were all superior. "I say yes to everything. Will you have them ready for brunch?"

They both nodded yes.

"Fabulous job, I hate to leave. The smells of peanut butter, chocolate, popcorn, and the casseroles are scrumptious. I'll call my friend at the paper and see if she will hand deliver our release to the advertising department so we can get it in tomorrow's paper. Thank you so much. Please pass the rest of those treats out to the staff. If you get any negative feedback, which I whole heartedly doubt, let me know."

Wednesday, the place was a madhouse. Chief Keith Wesley came in for dinner with Randy. I went over to say hi. Randy seemed thrilled. Wesley acted so cold I checked his nose for icicles. The man seriously had no use for me.

I stepped in to help the waitresses fill glasses and bus tables. We stayed behind the entire night. By the time we had it cleaned up and counted the money we were more than ready to call it a day. My last official duty was to put the money in the floor safe. We made a rule years before. Nobody went to the bank at night. National Security Company came once a week, signed for the money and left the change we needed.

Tried and true fifty-year-old habits helped the business run smoothly.

CHAPTER TWELVE

Nutmeg growled two or three times during the night. I dutifully got up each time and checked on Mother's apartment. I went downstairs, closed my eyes, and put my ear to her door. No noise or lights came from the inside. I went upstairs and climbed back into bed.

The temperature was unseasonably warm. I had decided to sleep with my window open. I lived on the second floor with no fire escape. The ladder I needed to throw out the window in case of emergency laid neatly folded under said window.

Nutmeg ran to the window, jumped up, and put both paws on the sill.

I rolled out of bed, crawled over and peeked out cautiously. Two cops proceeded to go through the trash bins from Moonstone Lake Café. I turned around and slid to a sitting position with my back to the wall.

I took three deep breaths to get my temper under control. How dare Wesley have my trash searched.

A minute or two later, once I calmed, I thought, *this is crap*. I stood, leaned out the window as far as I could and yelled down, "If you're hungry I'll open the kitchen and fix you something to eat."

Both men looked up at me and without a word, they dusted off their uniforms, got into their car, and left.

Aunt Sandra and I must have moved up on the suspect list.

Sandy didn't kill her and I certainly didn't do it. Jake Anderson could not have done it. He didn't get close enough to slip her a Mickey. Besides, he didn't plan anything, he reacted like he did at Sunday Brunch. I took my list of suspects and crossed him off. Sandra and I had put a strike through our names when we first made the list.

We were down to Michael, the three Young's, and the two Freedman men. I added Sherri Stein from the Bud and Bloom Flower Shop. She had the flower contract and I'd bet my last dollar Ruth treated her the same way she had treated us.

I found it difficult to sleep after the police incident. When I got up, Nutmeg and I went on our morning jog. I noticed people had an odd manner around dogs. Some stayed behind me. The runners who came toward me left the path and ran in the grass until they were safely around my dog. She didn't notice any of them.

I showered and put on a skirt and sweater. A leisurely dinner with Liz would be fun, and maybe informative.

I sat on the bed and opened the bottom drawer of my nightstand to pick out a scarf. As I searched for one I came across five different weekly planners. Would I ever get organized?

My life had become too predictable for me to worry about a schedule. Jog, shower, read, play with the dog, go to work, talk to Mother or Sandy, and go to bed. Sleep and repeat. Maybe I'd take up basket weaving. My life slipped into a boring routine.

I thought about the murders I'd helped solve with the old chief, Paul Chase. I figured out a majority of the clues with him and he had appreciated it.

Chief Keith Wesley was pompous, conceited, and closed minded. I would have paid money to have Paul Chase move back to Moonstone Lake.

I went in early to do the preliminaries and talk to the staff. It didn't happen often, but someone left a derogatory note on the cashier's table before they left the night before. One of my wait staff had made a rude comment or gesture to a patron.

I knew the guilty party. She had worked for me for three years and had two small children. Her mother babysat so she could work. I also knew customers were not always right. "Hey, guys and gals, I am blessed every day you all come here and work so hard to make this place a success. We were busy last night and people get antsy to have their glass filled or more butter on the table.

"I have told you before. If someone treats you poorly or talks to you in a way you think is demeaning, come to me. Don't take the chance of losing your job over an incident you had no control over. Thanks for all you do. We are about to open. Have a great day."

April Hill lowered her head slightly and I knew I had guessed right. I smiled at her as she went by.

I trailed out after the crew and there stood Mother. She walked from table to table. She smiled and chatted with everyone. The guests loved to see her. I leaned toward my aunt and asked. "Is she dressed?"

She handed me a piece of paper. "Here, these are the changes your mother wants you to make. I looked it over. The entire list would take around two years and a hundred thousand dollars. Better think of something to tell her, because here she comes." Aunt Sandy said.

"Arizona, don't you come to work on time? What is that mangy dog doing under the cashier's table?"

"Do you want me to answer those in order?" Since I meant it to be flip, I continued. "I've been in back with the crew. Now and then, they need a pep talk. As for the dog, she keeps us from being robbed."

"We've never been robbed."

I grinned. "See, it works. And rest easy knowing I'll give your suggestions the attention they deserve. What are your plans for the day?"

Mom shook her head at me. "I'm going to go home and worry about you running this restaurant into the ground."

"Don't do that, Mother. I had the best teacher in the world. You deserve a rest. I hear they play cards every day at the Senior Center. They take trips to the casinos, and you can eat there."

She looked me up and down. "At the present time I don't need a social director, but if I do, I'll call you."

Liz showed up for dinner around seven. James fixed us a shrimp dinner with baked potato and a Caesar salad. For dessert Lewis brought out Banana's Foster, my favorite.

We shared a bottle of Moscato I picked up from Danny's Bar and Grill the day before. Moonstone Lake Café didn't have a liquor license. To have a hundred different personalities on weekdays and sometimes five hundred at Sunday Brunch proved difficult enough. We certainly didn't need wine, beer, and mixed drinks thrown in the mix.

Liz leaned back in her chair and put her hands on her belly. "Ary, I envy you. You never gain weight. You look the same size as you were in college, in high school, for that matter. I, on the other hand, could skip the eating part and just rub the food on my belly and thighs. It goes there anyway."

"I don't stay this skinny because I want to. I dream about having more curves and fewer angles on my body."

She glanced toward the front of the diner where Sandra sat to count the drawer. "Your mom and Aunt are not skinny. Sandy looks fabulous, but your mom, not so much."

We broke out in laughter. It was as though the last three years had never happened. "You do remember she is not my real mom, don't you? "

"I didn't forget. I know it's hard for you."

I wiped the laughter tears from my eyes. "I can't forget she adopted me to keep the business. It always goes to the oldest daughter. She didn't have any children, so she went out and bought one."

"Oh, Ary, I'm sure there was more to it than that. She sent you to college, and gave you the restaurant."

"She didn't actually leave it to me. She didn't want to break a four generation line of ownership. It would have gone to her brother's son and then go from the oldest boy to the oldest boy. She couldn't let it happen. You know I don't think she was a bad mom. She's good to me. It's difficult when I want to know about my non-existent relatives.

"Nurturing is not in Emma's skill set. Had it not been for Aunt Sandra, I'd have a totally different personality than I have now. I couldn't remember one time I asked her to listen to me or help me that she didn't make time to do it. Mother never had or made time for me unless it helped with this place.

"She sent me to the doctor in the sixth grade to find out why I never got any heavier. He took a bunch of tests, and determined it was genetic. Since we had no idea who my real parents were, no one ever did anything." I changed the subject to Ruth Freedman. "Have you heard anything else about the murder case?"

It might have been the two glasses of wine that loosened her tongue. "I do know they are searching Young's house, the bakery, the flower shop, here, and the FBI is at the Freedman house in Boston."

"What are they looking for?"

"Poison, cyanide maybe, no one knows for sure. I heard it might not be anything. They won't say for sure. I got the sense they had no idea what it was. The medical examiner is checking with his colleagues. I heard Keith say he thought she died of a heart attack. My personal opinion is the authorities are using it as a reason to search everywhere."

I looked at her and shook my head. "It sounds lame and wrong to me."

I did my best not to rush the rest of our visit, yet I wanted to talk to James and Lewis, about poison. The way the chief treated me, I didn't want to give him a reason to suspect me more than he did. "How do you know this?"

She stood and slipped a light shawl over her shoulders. "I went to get the details on an accident. No one realized I was there. The Chief and some FBI agent talked in the hall."

"Why is the FBI involved?" I asked.

"Because two of the suspects live in Boston, I also found out the wedding is going on as planned. Haven't they called you?"

"About the wedding or the poison?"

"Both, I guess."

"No, neither."

Liz lived above The Hoof and Mane Beauty Shop on the Boardwalk. She walked home. I stood outside, breathed the fresh lake air and watched as Nutmeg escorted her. Within minutes, my dog came back to sit beside me.

I remembered her beautiful house on the north side on the lake. She'd had to sell it after Mick was arrested.

CHAPTER THIRTEEN

I hurried back to the kitchen. "Do you guys have time to talk a minute?

"Sure," they said in unison

We sat at the table in the kitchen. I directed my question to both chefs. "Do we have any cyanide in the building?"

James scratched his head. "We don't use any chemicals. You know we break all the equipment down at the end of the day and clean it. Did someone complain about bugs?"

I looked him in the eye. "Do you remember the Freedman lady? They found her in the lake but she didn't drown, she was poisoned." I didn't want to give them all the information Liz told me. I was confused enough about what it might be or might not be. Did Chief Keith Wesley use false facts to move his investigation along? I hoped I was wrong.

Lewis spoke up. "Too much of that stuff will kill

you, from what I have read, it's not an easy death. There's none here. Anymore it's mostly watered down and used to kill bugs on plants."

"Thanks, the police are coming here to see if we have any. I wanted a heads up in case we use it for something."

James lowered his head, but said nothing.

Sherri Stein owner of the Bud and Bloom moved up on my suspect list.

By the time I took Nutmeg out for her last walk, took a shower, and got into bed, exhaustion had taken over.

The first few weeks the dog slept on the floor. When I awoke the next day she would be in bed with me. When I didn't fuss at her she no longer pretended to sleep on the floor.

The moment I turned the light out, she took her place on the bed with her head on the empty pillow. She'd gained weight and was up to eighty-seven pounds.

The entire Boardwalk knew Nutmeg and loved her. She visited each shop except those with open food. The Health Department frowned on her being a visitor in those.

Tourists, like runners, stayed away from her although she never growled, barked, or acted the least bit aggressive. She did have a lead but I never made her wear it. I hoped Keith didn't pick up on it and make her use one. She never got a step in front of me. She heeled like a trained dog.

She had become my best friend.

I slept in which was unusual for me. I dreamt of cyanide, dead bodies and prison cells and didn't fall asleep until after three in the morning.

Once I checked the kitchen, I took a fresh pot of regular coffee in one hand and a decaf in the other and started around the dining room to see who had dropped by for breakfast.

There were more people than seats. The waiting line ran out the door and spilled onto the sidewalk. Patty Wolfram, one of the waitresses, seated folks while Sandra worked as cashier.

I didn't notice Chief Wesley among the crowd until I stood in front of his table. "Well, Chief, couldn't find a breakfast partner today?"

He pointed to the bench on the other side of the booth. "No, sit and have a cup of coffee with me."

"I sat one of the carafes down on the table top. "Thanks, but as you can see, we're busy. Did you want to question me again?" I didn't let him answer. "I have nothing new to add. Do you know if I murdered everyone who acted up in this place, I'd be in the hundreds, maybe thousands by now?"

I picked up the coffee and watched as his face turned red. I didn't know if it was anger or embarrassment, secretly I grinned inside.

Several times I glanced over to see if he had left. I would have bet he would finish his breakfast. He wouldn't dare put his manhood in jeopardy. He had to stay to prove what I said didn't bother him.

The coffee pots were empty. I went to the serving station for refills. By the time I returned, he was gone.

I didn't mind serving coffee. Pride of ownership made each and every job less of a hassle than if I worked for someone.

A lady sat in a booth alone at the back of the room. She had papers laid out in front of her. I offered her coffee. She looked up. Sherri Stein from Bud and Bloom sat in front of me. "My goodness, you look busy."

"Ary, sit down. Surely you have time for a cup of coffee."

I waved to Benny and pointed to the pots. As I sat, he turned my cup right side up and filled it. He warmed up Sherri's and left us to talk. "Sherri, I wish I saw more of you. I only think of buying flowers for weddings and funerals. If everyone was like me, you'd starve."

She became serious. "Did the police come to talk to you? They told me they were visiting everyone who had anything to do with Stacy's wedding. That's what I'm doing here. I'm trying to prove I have no cyanide now nor have I ever used it. The new police chief needs to learn some manners. One of his deputies told me they didn't even know if it was cyanide. They knew she didn't drown is all I got out of the conversation."

I took a sip of my coffee. "Why would you need cyanide? I also heard they were not even sure what kind of poison it was. I wonder if the new chief is trying to use this case to make a name for himself. The way he is going about it, the name he's building isn't one you can use in polite company."

She smiled, but it didn't reach her eyes. "Some florists use it to keep bugs off their flowers. I tried to tell him I don't use Styrofoam, plastic straws, or plastic water bottles. On my flowers, I use nothing stronger than Safer Soap."

Benny dropped back by to warm our coffee. I put my hand on hers as a gesture of understanding. "How about a pastry? I'm going to have an apple turnover. Lewis is a brilliant pastry chef. It might be just what you need," I spoke to our waiter. "Benny, bring two apple turnovers and we would like them warm and cinnamon ice cream on a separate dish."

I turned my attention back to the owner of the Bud and Bloom. "The chief needs a Dale Carnegie Course. I believe anyone in this town who had any contact with Mrs. Freedman is on his suspect list. Don't repeat this, but the poison angle might be a ruse to get access to our businesses and insinuate himself in our lives."

She pushed more of her papers out of the way. "Is that legal? Why me anyway? I never met the lady. Stacy and Dillon came to the shop alone. They picked out all of the flowers and table decorations. When we were almost finished, Denise Young came by and looked at everything. She loved what they chose and didn't make any changes. I don't know when Mrs. Freeman came to town, but she didn't come to see me."

"I'm going to call a friend of mine later and ask if all of this snooping the chief is doing is on the up and up,"" I said.

Benny sat the food on the table, I asked for a glass of water for each of us. "So you're telling me the chief is questioning you, searching your shop, and scouring through your invoices and you never met the victim?"

"That's exactly what I'm telling you."

"Amazing, is there anything I can do to help?

Have they searched your shop yet?"

She began to gather the papers and stack them. "I don't know why, but I think he wants to surprise me. I get the impression he's trying to railroad me. I can't for the life of me figure out why."

She put her papers in her briefcase. I could tell she wanted to leave. "Let me have Benny put that turnover in a to-go box. It'll taste pretty good for a snack later when you aren't as stressed."

She nodded yes. "I guess you know the wedding is four weeks from Saturday. I wish I had never heard of this wedding party." She stood and began to cry. Before she spoke again, she looked around to see who might be within hearing range. "I escaped a bad marriage seven years ago and came here. I changed my name and didn't even tell my parents, my friends, or my sister where I am. If I get any publicity and my ex-husband, Roy, finds me then all of my hard work and loneliness has been in vain. I'm not sure Roy wouldn't come after me, or worse."

"Do you want me to go with you tomorrow to talk to Chief Wesley? Explain the situation."

"No, Ary. What if he's the kind of man who would taunt me with the information? Thanks for the talk. I needed it. I'll let you know what happens. Right now I'm trying to convince him I don't use any chemicals. I don't know why he doesn't talk to the bride and groom. They know I never met Ruth Freedman."

Sandra wanted to take off from eleven to three to have lunch with an old school chum in town. It would be a long day. By eleven-thirty, the entire crew had arrived.

I took time to go home and try to reach Chief Paul Chase. He answered on the third ring, "Hi Chief, this is Arizona Summers."

"I recognized your voice. How's the restaurant business?"

"Busy. Do you like your new job?"

"Yes, but once in a while I miss the lake and the quiet. I know you didn't call to chat. What can I do for you?"

I took a deep breath. "There was a murder here last month."

"I heard about that. Are you and Keith working together to solve it?"

"Not really. That's why I called. The woman was found in the lake but there was no water in her lungs. First we heard she might have been poisoned and thrown in the water. Now I find out it might not be true. Chief Wesley is using the poison angle as a reason to make every person the woman met a suspect. Can he do that?"

"It's unfortunate for innocent people, Arizona, but cops can lie. There's nothing to say they have to tell the truth or give all information they know if it will help them catch the bad guy."

I didn't know what to say.

"Ary, are you there."

"Yes I'm here. Is there a chance she had a foreign substance in her body and they can't identify it?"

"Your question is what can be detected in a body after is has been in the water? Here is something most people don't know. If a person drowns in fresh water and takes in small amounts of the water at a time, they can drown and not have water in the lungs."

"I won't keep you Chief. Thanks for the help."

"I hope Keith loosens up. He's missing out not including you in his work.

"Don't judge him too harshly. No matter how much a person learns in the class room, cases come up you never knew were possible. I spent time with him when I turned the station over. He's a decent guy."

"I'll keep that in mind. Thanks again for your help."

"You're welcome feel free to call any time."

CHAPTER FOURTEEN

I washed my hands, brushed my teeth and hair and headed downstairs to the restaurant. I ran smack into Mother. Nutmeg lay under the cashier's stand as usual. If I got lucky, she wouldn't see her or remember I had a dog. "Arizona. Come here."

I went.

"Arizona. I want the dining room painted. This is the color I picked out."

I was at a loss for words. I had an unwritten rule, never paint anything in a color you can describe by referencing the color of a piece of farm equipment.

To get my thoughts aligned before I said the wrong thing, I guided her toward the kitchen. "Would you like to try some of the new dishes James and Lewis made for the buffet? We have peanut butter and chocolate."

"Goodness girl, I hope you haven't tried to clone a Reese's Peanut Butter Cup. I'm too old to go to jail."

"No one's going to put you in jail, Mom."

She followed me but fussed the entire time. "Lewis could you get my mother a dish of peanut butter balls and a glass of milk."

"Lewis. Don't you dare put a dessert on the buffet called peanut butter balls."

As he sat the dish in front of her he tried not to laugh but he couldn't help himself. "Emma, we call them peanut butter nuggets. They're delicious, try one."

She put an entire two-inch ball in her mouth. I held my breath until she came up for air. I handed her the milk. "Here, take a drink. You realize we painted last summer. Our budget isn't set up to paint again so soon."

She looked around the room as though the person she wanted to speak to might be hiding under the stove or refrigerator. "Where's Sandra? She knows when we last painted. I swear Arizona you're too young to lose your memory."

"She went to the city for lunch."

"You girls, we live and work in the food business and she wants to go elsewhere for a meal?"

I crossed my arms over my chest. "Sometimes it isn't the food, it's the company."

She laid a small square of paper on the table. "Horse hockey, come take a look at this paint sample."

"You had me look at them when you came in."

While she scarfed down more nuggets, I thought my words over carefully. "Emma, there's nothing soothing about John Deere green or Mary Kay pink in an eating establishment. It'll look like the set of a child's television program."

She yelled for the Chefs. "James, Lewis, come over here and look at this color scheme I've picked out and give me your honest opinion."

Both looked at me and rolled their eyes. They could recognize a no-win situation when they saw one. James began. "Emma, the pink is a nice color, but it looks too much like bubble gum, maybe something lighter." He had talked himself into a corner. "I'd have to say about a hundred shades lighter, the same with the green."

Lewis lowered his head and gave her a flat-eyed stare. "I have to agree with James, ma'am."

"You people have no taste. She picked up the dish of candy and prepared to take it with her. She scuffed toward the kitchen door in her fuzzy leopard spotted slippers, bright red slacks and green cardigan. Right before she stepped into the hall, she turned back and stuck her tongue out at us.

The rest of the day turned out to be pleasant. I relayed Mom's behavior about the paint and food to Sandra when she returned from her outing.

She shook her head. "Maybe we should take some snacks to her apartment and play cards. She would like it. What we used to do on Wednesday nights, we rarely do at all. Maybe she acts up because she feels neglected."

"Good idea."

Once we closed the café and put the money in the safe, James fixed a platter of ham, cheese, and homemade bread. Lewis stacked another tray with different desserts. We all knew what she liked best.

Sandra sat on a stool behind me. "What do you think she'll do when she sees Nutmeg?"

I picked up one tray of food and handed the other to her. "I never thought about it."

"My idea would be to leave the dog outside until she realizes we came to spend the evening. Once we begin to play cards, open the door and let her in. Maybe Emma won't notice."

I shook my head. "Yeah, sure."

We knocked on Mom's door about nine-thirty. I doubt she could hear us over the sound of the TV. Sandra opened the door and went in first. "Emma, we came to play cards."

She turned off the television set and looked back toward the door. "Don't be a chicken, Arizona. Come on in."

I regretted the plan already and we hadn't sat down yet. I let Nutmeg go in. She walked over to the couch and laid down on the floor at the end.

Mother watched her every step but said nothing. We sat the food on her kitchen counter and opened a bottle of wine we found in her fridge. Mom opened the food containers and began to eat. She chose a piece of coconut pie. "To what do I owe this visit? Finally feel bad about leaving the old lady alone twenty-four-seven?"

We looked at one another but didn't acknowledge her questions.

Once we began a game of Canasta, Sandra looked at me and nodded her head. I took the queue and mentioned the senior citizens again. "Mom, the paper had an article about the new Senior Citizen's building on the north side. They have quilting, cards, group tours, cruises, jam sessions, and so many more events I can't remember all of them. A lot of the ladies, who used to come in for lunch, now eat at the Senior Center. I heard there are chess and checker games all the time. Are you interested?"

Sandra took a five of hearts from the discard pile, added six more from her hand and laid them on the table.

"I'm not any more interested than I was last time you mentioned it." She looked from Sandra to me. Crossed her arms and stopped eating. "Well, get to the real reason you keep bringing this up."

"We might be worried about how much time you spend alone. Food has become your best friend. Mainly we are thinking about you. You sit and watch the television for hours at a time. You haven't been for a walk for ages. It's time to do something good for yourself."

Emma drew and discarded, and poured her second glass of wine. With wine comes courage, not necessarily wisdom. "How would I get to the north side?"

"They have buses every two hours. They are free if you're over sixty-five," Sandy answered as she laid down her last book for cards and said Canasta.

Mother stood, walked to the door and opened it for us to leave. "I'll think about it. I don't like old people. And if I eat there it will be one more person not eating at the café."

"Don't worry about that part of it Mother. You don't pay anyway."

CHAPTER FIFTEEN

Daylight savings time began. I adjusted my run to six a.m. I stretched on the bench outside the four-plex. Nutmeg stretched too. She cracked me up. She put both paws on the bench and lowered her head to the sidewalk.

Instead of heading home when we were finished, we walked off the trail and onto the Boardwalk.

Most shops opened at ten and closed at six in the evening. During tourist season they opened at the same time but stayed open until ten so people could have time to shop and still spend the day on the lake.

The street had yet to come alive except for the Bud and Bloom. Three police cars with lights flashing lit the street. I knew I wouldn't be welcome, but I went inside the shop anyway.

Sherri sat at a table in the back and faced me. Keith Wesley sat across from her, his back to me. I walked up as if I belonged. "Hi, Sherri, what happened, were you robbed?"

Keith turned around. "What are you doing here?"

Nutmeg growled and her hackles ruffled.

"Take that dog out of here." He ordered.

Sherri patted the seat of the chair beside her. "No, I would like them to stay. I feel safer with them here."

He looked straight at her. "How could you not feel safe? There are four police officers and two crime scene detectives here. You couldn't be more protected."

Sherri looked at me, so I spoke up. "Miss Stein would like to see your warrant and probability cause statement. You can produce them, can't you, Chief? We'd like to read your reasoning behind this search and the name of the judge who signed the warrant."

He stood. "Men, we are done here. Pack up and let's go." He put his palms on the table and leaned down so we were eye to eye. "Arizona Summers; I told you not to interfere in police business. I meant it."

"I'm not interfering Keith. I'm making sure your techniques are by the book. It is obviously a good thing I did. I won't get into your murder investigation, and you don't step on people's rights. Does that work for you?"

He balled his hands into fists but left them by his sides. "It's Chief Wesley to you. Don't presume we are friends."

I stood. "Oh, Keith, I would never make that mistake. You had better hurry. Your men are waiting for you outside."

He looked at Sherri. "Miss Stein, I believe you

should pick some new friends. This one could get you in trouble."

I sat and relaxed into my chair. "Glad that's over. Do you think he was mad?"

We both laughed. "How do you know all that stuff?" She asked.

"I wasn't sure. I saw it on an episode of Law and Order. I'm sure glad it was true."

I stayed and helped Sherri put the shop back in order. She turned out to be a funny and delightful woman. I had made a new friend."

Sandy wasn't at work so Nutmeg and I went to her apartment. She answered the door with a book in her hand. "What are you reading?"

She glanced down at the book. "A cozy mystery, this is book eight in a series. I love them. You should read more. It's calming. You can't have your mind on a story and worry about anything else. It's like meditation to me."

She stood back so I could step inside. "You know, Aunt Sandy, if you get tired of café work, you could advertise for bookstores."

As Nutmeg crossed the threshold, all three cats jumped off the couch and began to weave in and out her legs and rub on her fur. She quickly laid down. They all climbed on her and kneaded her fur to make beds. Sandy and I stood and watched.

I went in, opened the fridge and took a soda. "I stopped to tell you what happened at the Bud and Bloom."

I tried to stick to the facts. People who knew me said I embellished stories. I preferred to say I added a few adjectives to make it more interesting to the listener.

Sandra got out her copy of our suspect list and crossed off Sherri Stein. We were back to the Young's, Mr. Freedman, Dillon, and Stacy.

As I got ready to leave, Sandy said, "Do you think it could be some random person we don't know about? She alienated everyone she met. Maybe you should talk to the bride and groom to see if they can think of anyone we don't have on the list."

What a great idea. I had no time to pursue it at the moment. It was after eleven and I had not as yet made an appearance at the café. If the truth be told, I could have been gone months and it would all run smoothly. Mother didn't want people to know that. If they did, she would have been irrelevant.

The evening turned out as most did, with a screaming baby, two or three kids who ran between tables while their parents completely ignored them and one person who had a complaint about the food so they didn't have to pay the bill. Those gripes usually came from people who ordered the most expensive items on the menu and ate every bite before they complained.

The high point came when four friends of mine from high school walked in, Sara Brock, Danielle Mason, Bobbie Brand, and Audrey Sampson. They were in town for their fifteenth class reunion.

Bobbie greeted me. "Oh my goodness, Ary, so good to see you. Can you sit with us?"

I glanced around the dining room and at the clock. We were almost cleared out. "Sure, I'd love to hear what you all have been doing."

They were a year ahead of me in school. We ran

cross-country track together.

Danielle patted my hand. "Look at you, the restaurant owner. Do you like it?"

I signaled for Jill to bring water and menus. "It has its moments, like now. It isn't like I missed something else I wanted to do. I was raised to take over here, no ifs, ands, or buts. What are the rest of you up to? Audrey, did you marry Danny Mann?"

"Yes, I did. We've been married thirteen years."

After the drink order, I asked, "any kids?"

"Yes, we have a boy, almost fourteen."

Sara chimed in, "do the math."

We all laughed and bantered back and forth until the food came. Danielle had become a lawyer. "We hear you had a murder in Moonstone Lake."

It surprised me they would know. "Did we make the National news?"

"No, Dillon Freedman was a junior associate at the law firm I work for in Boston. He's been out for a few weeks because of his mother and the wedding. He'll be happy when he gets back. They moved him up a step."

I had to ask, "Did you ever meet his mother?"

"Gad, yes. What a witch. No one liked her. She came to work one time and demanded Dillon be given a raise. He was humiliated. If he hadn't been such a good lawyer, they would have fired him so they didn't have to deal with her again."

"Oh, Danielle that's terrible."

Once I heard about his mom, my mind dropped out of the conversation. I mentally moved Dillon up on the suspect list.

Benny tapped me on the shoulder. "You have a

visitor."

I stood and turned around. Police Chief Keith Wesley stood by the door with his hat in his hand.

I excused myself and went over to where he stood. "What can I do for you?"

"Ary, can you step outside a minute?"

My heart jumped to my throat. Nutmeg took a step closer to him and let out a warning bark. I'd never heard her do that before.

"Can you call her off? I didn't come here to harass you."

I put my hand up and Nutmeg took two steps back. She didn't take her eyes off the chief.

He opened the door and the three of us went out. He walked until he came to the bench under the hackberry tree in front of my apartment building. "Sit down."

Nutmeg sat on the ground facing us with her head between us. "Arizona, please." He looked at the dog.

"Nutmeg; by me. What can I do for you, Chief Wesley?

He turned toward me. "I came to apologize for my behavior."

I hadn't expected him to say he was sorry. "For accusing me of killing Ruth Freedman, for the way you talked to me about sticking my nose into police business, or the way you acted at the Bud and Bloom?"

"You're a hard woman, Arizona. I'm sorry for all of it. We all like to be popular, especially the new guy. I had big shoes to fill. Paul Chase was a saint in this town."

"You picked a backward way to do it. Did you

learn the old saying *you can catch more flies with honey than with vinegar?"*

He stood, so I did too. He took my face in both of his hands and pulled me to him. My heartbeat quickened. We were about to have a moment. I couldn't believe it. Nutmeg sat by my foot and stared at Keith.

He leaned down so our lips nearly touched. He bent my head down and kissed me on the forehead.

I had my eyes closed. It took a few seconds to absorb what had actually happened.

I stood like a statue. Dumbfounded, I cried, but not tears of shame or love, tears of anger. Nutmeg pulled on my shirt to try to have me sit again.

Had he grinned at me before he left or did I imagine it?

Once I heard the door close on his police cruiser, I threw a tantrum. I stomped, kicked, and yelled. He came to humiliate me. I would have bet money on it.

CHAPTER SIXTEEN

The Adventure Book Club met once a month, but it seemed to come around more quickly than that. We were to meet at Martha Adam's house on the north side of the lake. Earlier in the day, I had gotten the car out, dusted it off, and filled it with gas.

Once I established a routine in Moonstone Lake, I didn't use the car much. Most everything I did and the places I visited were within walking distance. The car became a necessity in the winter. The wind off the lake made for some mighty cold wind chills. In the summer the cool breeze made for relief on the warmest of days.

Sandra and Mother had keys also but neither one of them drove much more than I did.

I knew about the wind chill chart, maybe someone needed to invent a coolness chart guided by the light winds off of water. It could be named the Water Breeze Chart.

I joined the club because Aunt Sandra asked me. She said it was something Mom, she and I could do together. She was convinced it would entertain Mother, who loved to visit, try new food, and she read nearly as much as Sandra.

Every member took a dish to share and the hostess provided drinks. We were always welcome at events such as the book club. One of our chefs created a fabulous dish each month for us to take along. The high point for James and Lewis were the recipes we traded with the other members. For every dish the cook made copies of the recipe for us to take home. Some months there were fabulous finds, other months, not so much.

I parked the car in the lot and headed to the kitchen to check on the food. The smells of pumpkin and spices hit me as I entered the front door. I loved all things pumpkin, especially pumpkin latte, muffins, candles, and pie. "What have we here?" I asked as I entered the kitchen. "I know it has pumpkin in it."

Lewis pointed to a counter behind him. "A pumpkin spice Bundt cake. It's a damp and chilly night; pumpkin is always tasty on a cold night."

"My, Lewis, it's beautiful. I love that you sprinkled it with powdered sugar."

"Did you print out the recipe?"

"I certainly did. There are fifteen copies next to the cake." He turned toward the storage room. "I'll get a box. Who's working for you and Sandy tonight?"

"Matt will play hostess and cashier. Mark will help and make sure it flows. The regular crew will be here to serve. Will you and James take the receipts after the drawer is counted and put it all in the safe? As usual, don't open the safe in front of anyone but James. Where is James?"

"He had a funeral to attend. He'll be here before long. Everything is prepped. We can easily serve a hundred people. If someone orders an entrée we didn't anticipate, I can take care of it."

James at a funeral seemed odd. I had never heard him talk about anyone. More than once I wondered what he did every night.

"I'm sure you can. It seems like a lot for you to handle. Want me to stay?"

"No, you're a great cook, but James would be upset if he knew you missed your party because of him."

I thanked Lewis, told him how lucky the restaurant and, especially, me were to have him. Mom and Aunt Sandy were in the foyer when I came out of the kitchen. We were ready to go. Nutmeg stayed with Mike at the hostess podium.

I loved the food best. Ninety-eight percent of the time we ate at our own diner. Monthly potlucks were a treat.

Aunt Sandy thought Mom and I would embarrass her because we weren't prepared. "Tell me both of you read the book. People can tell if you're faking it."

Since Ruth Freedman's demise, my reading material had changed to forensics. "Actually, I did. I read it in college and it was good enough I still remembered it, maybe not every word, but when I began to read it again, the story flowed back to me."

Mom said nothing. Sandra tried again. "How about you, Emma, did you read the book?"

Mother looked out the window. I could see her breath. "Duh, I belong to the club to read books."

Five minutes later we walked into Martha's two story colonial, books in hand. Sandy had the cake and I helped Mom, not that she needed it, she reminded me three times on the way to the door. It was the daughterly thing to do. Aunt Sandy took the cake out of the box and gathered recipes from the other members.

I looked to see who showed up. There were fifteen in the club, but notoriously about eight members attended any one meeting, this night they expected eleven.

To my surprise, Denise Young had a cup of coffee and had taken a seat. I picked the one beside her. "Hi, Denise, how are you?"

She sat her cup on the table between us. "I have never dealt with someone being murdered before. It skews your idea of people. I feel as though I can't trust the people closest to me. It's a horrible feeling."

We stopped talking and greeted the members as they came in. I wondered if they came because they wanted to see if Denise was there and maybe get the inside skinny on the murder or on the off chance they enjoyed the book.

I knew human nature. I watched it play out every day at my job. I'd have bet the members came to see Denise first and discuss the book second.

We chatted for the first few minutes before Martha began the discussion by asking if everyone enjoyed the selection. Nine times out of ten, I didn't have time to read the book or it ended up to be a critic's choice. I had found anything the critics raved about, I usually didn't like.

Martha looked directly at me and waited for my response. I smiled and said it was my favorite so far. "The first time I read it was in college. At that time I had doubts about the format. The thought of reading boring letters didn't excite me. It was so well written I soon became interested in the story and forgot about the unusual format. It didn't hurt that I learned some history along the way."

Had my nose grown?

I didn't have to say another word. The discussion took off. I sat and observed Denise and her interaction with the other guests. She nodded and smiled, but said nothing.

The book review ended. We gathered around the fabulous food and filled our plates. I took a small serving of all the offerings. My favorites, besides the pumpkin cake included Italian meatballs in a tangy garlic and basil gravy with a beef stock base. I could have eaten the entire crock full. Another awesome dish, a cold salad had pulled chicken breast with finely chopped, grapes, apples, pecans, and celery added and blended together with mayonnaise and sour cream. Those were the two most popular. I notice the dishes were empty at the end of the evening.

The first question out of the chefs' mouths in the morning would be, *did you like the food? What was your favorite? This recipe looks interesting, did you try it?*

Denise and I sat back in the same chairs. When I

was small, we had the three second rule. If you left your seat for any more than three seconds, it became free and anyone could steal it from you. The ladies at Martha's house were more polite.

I tried to rekindle the conversation we started before the food was served. "About what you said earlier, you don't suspect anyone in your own family do you, Denise?"

She looked from side to side to see if anyone was close enough to hear. "I feel I can talk to you, lord knows I need to talk to someone. You dealt with Ruth once. Can you imagine dealing with her day after day for years? It makes me wonder if Dillon or his father, Roger, couldn't take it any longer and lost control." She took a choppy breath and kept talking. "Then there's Jackson. Every night when we got into bed he said, *I don't know how much more of this I can take. If it goes on much longer she'll drive me to commit murder*."

I tried to squelch her fears. "People say stuff like that all the time. They rarely mean it. Once the wedding is over, you and Jackson won't have to think about her again."

"Stacy had a fit one day and said *if Ruth makes one more rude comment I'm going to kill her.* I said, Stacy, don't say things like that and she said, *Mom, I mean it. I am about to snap*."

"Again, I doubt she meant it. It's what I call tough talk. It's spouting off over something that's out of your hands. It gives you a sense of power. Did you know Ruth went to Dillon's job in Boston and ask for a raise on his behalf?"

"Oh, Ary, that's the tip of the iceberg. To hear

Stacy tell it, she stepped in at little league, boy scouts, high school basketball, a college professor Dillon had a problem with, and the list goes on and on. It's why he and Stacy didn't want to go back to Boston to live."

"I heard a rumor he got a promotion since he's been here."

"I know, but he is going to go into Bart and Ryan as a full partner. His dad bought him in as a wedding present."

"That's a great deal of money."

"The Freedman's didn't have money problems, but something was going on between her and Roger. He remained angry with her all the time. Stacy thought it was the stress of the wedding. I didn't think so. I caught words like, *you stole, jail, how can we continue to live there?* I tell you, one to them is guilty of something and it was more than likely illegal."

I reached over and patted her knee lightly. "Who said the words you overheard, Roger or Ruth?"

"Roger. He seemed pleasant enough when we were all together but when they were alone, I thought they might have a knockdown drag-out fight." She smiled for the first time all evening. "I wasn't sure he could beat her in a fight. She had both a weight and a meanness advantage."

"Would you like me to look into it?

"Yes, Arizona, but how could you?"

"I have my resources."

"I don't know if this will help, but the reason Stacy and Dillon wanted the wedding here, was because Ruth runs a foundation in Boston. They were sure she would have to stay there most of the time to oversee it and would only be able to break away to come to the family wedding events. Boy, did they get fooled!"

Everyone left but Mom, Sandra, Denise, and me. Marsha Adams graciously cleared the tables with Sandy's help and left us alone to talk.

"Denise, we had better go and give Marsha her house back. If you need to talk again, come to the restaurant. I am nearly always there. I'd like to ask one more question."

Denise stood. "Sure, what?

"Were any of the people, you mentioned earlier, who knew Ruth had stepped into Dillon's life all those times in town the same time she was?"

"I'll have to think. No, I don't think so....wait, Mark O'Shay flew in for a weekend. He's Dillon's best friend, when they were teenagers Mark became so angry with Ruth, he tripped her. She fell and broke her nose. She was furious when she found out he would be best man."

"How long was he here?"

Marge brought Denise's jacket and helped her put it on, "Stacy and Dillon drove him to the airport in Branson and barely made it back to have brunch at your place"

"Arizona, do you think it's important?"

I shrugged my shoulders. "Honestly, I have no answers. It might be easier to figure out who didn't want her dead."

My mind raced at the possibilities but came to a screeching halt when I got to the car and Nutmeg sat beside it waiting for me. "Nutmeg, did you run all the way over here?"

Mother, already halfway seated in the passenger seat, stood and walked to the hood where she could look over at the dog. "She had better head back now because she's not riding in the same car as me."

"Yes, Mom, yes she is."

Sandra got out of the back seat where she rode on the way over. "One of you can sit back here with me."

Mother's face turned crimson and it wasn't from the cool damp night. "One of us? You two act like the dog is human."

Sandy and I looked at one another and smiled before I answered, "She might be."

Nutmeg didn't wait for an answer. She jumped in the back seat and snuggled in.

Mother made some sort of a comment under her breath. I couldn't understand it and I didn't dare ask her to repeat it.

"How far do you think it is from the apartments to Martha's house?" I answered my own question. "At least five miles, she is one loyal dog."

Nutmeg barked one time. Mother jumped.

Sandra and I walked Mom into her apartment and asked if she needed anything. Nutmeg, my Aunt and I went upstairs to her abode. The cats were thrilled to have her home, but even more thrilled to have Nutmeg to pester. She took it good-naturedly.

I took my jacket off and hung it on the doorknob. "Have any soda?"

"How about tea," she asked, "What were you and Denise in such a deep discussion about?"

I got up to retrieve her suspect list she kept on top

of the bookcase. I'd update mine when I got to the apartment. "We can take Denise Young off of it. She's so afraid one of her family killed Ruth. She gave me numerous reasons why it could have been any one of them, especially Stacy."

Sandy readjusted to make room for Wynken and Blynken on her lap. Nod stayed where he was, on Nutmeg's head. "How do you know she wasn't trying to throw suspicion on another person so she would look innocent?"

"Why would she care what I thought? I have no authority and I guarantee Chief Wesley doesn't want to hear my opinions."

I told her about the best man, Mark O'Shay. "He and Ruth Freedman had a long history of animosity toward one another. I'm crossing Denise off and adding Mark O'Shay. She said she thought there was trouble between Ruth and Roger. She had a feeling one of them had done something unsavory. From the fragment she overheard she is certain Ruth was the culprit."

"Arizona, are you telling me the Freedman's stayed at the Young's while Ruth went around insulting every person she met?"

Nod jumped off Nutmeg and wanted me to pick her up. "Yes. I know Mrs. Freedman ran some sort of foundation. I need to find out more about it, and I had no idea what Roger Freeman did for a living, but for some reason, stockbroker comes to mind."

Sandy yawned. "It's been four weeks. If it was an easy investigation, there would be a person in custody by now."

I finished my tea and put the cup in the kitchen

sink. "The first two weeks were wasted while you, me, and Sherri Stein were questioned and harassed. Any fresh clues were lost, wet, or blown away.

"Why didn't we look for clues? Any more you can find out all you want to know about any one if you search the right places on the internet. I didn't even look at her obituary. I'll do it tomorrow. Nutmeg and I are going for a walk, and then I'm off to bed."

The cats had gone back to bugging the dog. They ran toward Nutmeg and jumped like Halloween cats when they touched her. "You know. I never did understand the appeal of cats over dogs, but yours are entertaining."

CHAPTER SEVENTEEN

There's an old saying about Missouri. If you don't like the weather, hang around a few minutes, it'll change. It held true as I began my morning run. The sun shined brightly in a cloudless sky, and the winds had settled down.

Nutmeg and I followed our usual routine. When we finished, I headed down to the water's edge near where I first saw Mrs. Freedman's body. It had occurred to me several times, the body might not have moved much. The lake didn't have a current so the body would have to move with the wake from the boats.

They found the body on a Thursday. If it had been in the water three to four days, it would have been dumped on Monday or Tuesday. That would put it in the water the last of February. Daylight savings time didn't start until March eleventh.

I concluded only fishermen were on the lake. It

was too cold for recreational boating. Fishermen were not allowed to use gas engines; electric motors only. The wake would have been nearly undetectable. In my mind, the body would have stayed within a hundred yards east or west of where it was discovered. The north shore measured at least four miles at its closest point to the body.

I sat on what remained of a rock bench near the water. Mentally I marked off the distance I calculated it as the size of a football field and began to explore.

Nutmeg explored with me. We went west. I found a stick and prodded every shiny object or piece of paper I saw. If I missed anything, the dog pointed it out. We scoured the water's edge, the shoreline as far as hundred yards on the shore and twenty feet toward the sidewalk above us. We did the same going east. Thirty feet from our starting point, Nutmeg barked.

She ran in circles and pawed the ground. I went to her side, reached down to pick up her find. I held in my hand a plain gold band. It had an inscription on the inside. I couldn't read it because of the dirt and grime.

I jogged toward home.

For the first time, I noticed when Nutmeg was pleased or happy she held her head high and pranced. She kept her pose all the way to the apartments.

She had turned out to be the best friend I'd ever had and didn't know I needed.

After my shower, I dressed and headed downstairs to the kitchen. I left the recipes from the night before on my dresser. I went back to get them, and dropped the ring in my jeans pocket.

The two chefs, cook staff and the dishwasher were

already busy. They greeted me when I came in. James had a message for me. "Amy won't be able to make her shift today."

"Thanks. I need to hire at least two more servers." Not a week went by when everyone showed up. I walked over to the schedule board to check her hours. She had noon to six. I would work it. The other servers liked it when I worked. I put my tips on the desk and let them split the money at the end of the shift.

My tips were sometimes big because I was boss, other times they were nonexistent for the same reason.

I waved the recipes in the air. "Hey James, Lewis, have time for a cup of coffee?"

They met me at the counter. Lewis carried three mugs and James a carafe of coffee. I passed out the papers. "Four savory dishes and eight desserts."

James looked at his. "Every time you go to one of these things, the desserts outweigh the savory dishes two to one."

Lewis poured the coffee as we talked, "Sugar fans outnumber savory folks four to one."

We laughed and sipped our coffee. "How did last night go, any big problems?"

Lewis answered, "We had a great night. No boss to bug us or get in the way."

James playfully slapped Lewis with the recipes. "They had it under control when I got back. We couldn't get the safe open so we hid the money in the back alley behind the dumpster.'

I looked toward James. "Sorry about whoever died. Was it a friend or a relative?"

He had a deer in the headlights look on his face. I began to wonder if he intended to answer. "It was just a guy I talked to at the lake. No big deal."

"There is one thing. Lewis said. "It's that time of year when we usually change some of the sweet desserts for more fresh fruit and the hot dishes for more salad."

I stood. "How about you two getting it together, figure your costs and we can talk about it when you're ready."

I reached in my pocket and pulled out the ring. "James, do you know of any way I can clean this ring so I can read the inscription?"

He reached out and I sat the ring in the palm of his hand. "We can try rubbing it with aluminum foil. It works most of the time. If not, Albert's Jewelry and Pawn has a cleaner. Do you have any ideas Lewis?"

"If the aluminum foil doesn't work we can try vinegar."

Five minutes later, I had a shiny wedding ring in my hand. I stuck it back in my pocket to deal with later.

Thursday's were notoriously slow. Sandy had the day off. Benny and I had the entire floor with the help of one busboy. We would take our own orders, hang them in the window, serve them, ring them up when the folks were ready to go, and help bus the tables.

Had Amy come to work, I would have helped bus, serve, and handled the cash register. Oh, well, might as well deal with it.

I took sections one and two, Benny took three and four. Stan and Patty offered to stay over. They had been there since five am. They looked exhausted. If the two of them could do breakfast, Benny and I could work lunch and early dinner.

Right off the bat, Keith Wesley and Randy Malone came in and sat in my section. I took a deep breath and headed over. "What can I get for our esteemed police this afternoon?"

Ricky smiled and ordered. Keith didn't look up from his menu. "I'll take the lunch special with extra cheese. Can you bring me water with lemon and a chocolate shake?"

The Chief had no intention of looking my way. By golly, I could wait him out. Finally, "I'll take the same, but no extra cheese and I'll have a Coke."

I took their drinks back and set them on the table. They were deep in conversation. I overheard a few words before they realized I was back…*we can't do much until they come back for the wedding, but I still think he killed her…"*

They said he. I had been right. They didn't suspect Denise or Stacy Young. The Freedman men, Jackson Young, and Mark O'Shay, unless there happened to be another person I didn't know about. The number of suspects shrunk again.

The lunch crowd came in and out in a steady flow. Benny and I didn't have any problems. My feelings were not hurt when the dinner help came in and took over. My feet were about to betray me.

My tips were a goodly sum. Benny said I earned it and I should keep the money. The second time I told him it was his, he didn't argue. He went home a happy man.

Sandy came in the front door as Benny walked out the back. "Thought you might want some help, I'm rested and ready to go."

I walked with her to the hostess podium. I smiled when I realized Nutmeg had tucked herself out of sight under it. It didn't take her long to learn anything. "I found a ring on the shore this morning."

"Really, what kind of ring?"

"I think it's a wedding ring. It says something inside but I couldn't read it. I'll try again when I get upstairs. I don't want to take it out here. I'm going home to take a shower. I need to get off my feet for a half an hour. I'll be back. Thanks for coming in. Nutmeg, are you coming with me."

Of course.

I took a shower and put on a pale yellow form fitting sun dress and a sweater to match. I looked in the mirror. I didn't care what they said. I had curves, although they were small.

The ring lay on my dresser. I had to look at it before I went back to work.

Old jewelry had been a hobby at one time. During the season there were garage sales every day. People didn't know what they had. I scouted for gold, now and then I came across a diamond ring or broach. I kept a jewelry loupe in my desk.

As I thought about it, the memories of how much fun I had collecting jewelry flooded my mind and warm weather was around the corner.

Garage sales fascinated me. Matt from Albert's Jewelry and Pawn store of the same name bought my better finds. Every week I had extra money. Money wasn't a problem for me. The garage sale items were like when I looked down and found a dime. They meant more than the dimes I earned.

Money didn't bother me because I rarely had time to spend it. In a week, I worked sixty hours and dropped in on the restaurant another twenty.

If I wanted clothes I went to the north side. Groceries were a non-issue. James sent food up with us each night and Lewis always had an extra dessert or two. Mom ate downstairs in the dining room. Inevitably, one of her friends dropped by to eat with her, I'm sure it had nothing to do with the fact they ate free.

Nutmeg was the best fed dog in Moonstone Lake. Lewis had looked up all the foods she could eat. He added them together and cooked her gourmet dog food. He went so far as to bake a huge batch of dog biscuits when she began to run low.

Aunt Sandy bought at least three books a week. While I tried my best to read the book club selections every month.

I was about to join the audio book club so I could listen to books while I ran.

I pulled my desk lamp close and put the loupe up to my eye. On the outside, the ring had no distinguishing marks. The inside had an inscription, *Ruth love Roger 06/15/86 forever.*

Should I give the ring to the Chief? To me, it answered a question. She did not have it on when she went into the water. Bodies in the water got bigger, not smaller so the ring couldn't have fallen off.

Did someone take it off her finger to keep for sentimental reasons? Each clue I found made the murder more confusing. Why poison her if you were going to drown her? Could the poison have been an accident? I didn't remember if anyone said what kind of poison it was for sure. I decided to go with Paul Chase's explanation that she inhaled a substance in the water and it stayed in her body.

When I solved the other murders in Moonstone Lake, I had a primacies or scenario. I couldn't possibly do it in the current murder because I had no information I didn't dig up myself. Keith had my hands tied.

CHAPTER EIGHTEEN

The only way to find out if the old chief had the right idea would be for me to go to Stanfield and talk to the medical examiner, Dr. Marshall Stone.

With the ring safely in my desk drawer, I headed back to work. As I closed my apartment door, I turned back and chastised myself for the messes I made and didn't clean up. If I cleaned one room a night, it would be clean in six days.

The four apartments in the building each had two bedrooms, two baths, kitchen and living room. When one bedroom became too cluttered I didn't clean it. I moved to the second one. When they were both too disgusting to live in, I cleaned the empty one and moved back to it.

On the way back to the café' I promised myself I would clean it, all of it, and soon.

The last of the night's diners had coffee or dessert in front of them when I arrived.

Sandra moved to the cashier's table. Before I could announce my presence, Nutmeg pushed her way under the table. Aunt Sandra turned around to see me. "Well, did you find anything on the ring?"

"Yes, the engraving says *Ruth love Roger 06/15/86, forever.*

She bent her arms and put both hands over her mouth. "What do you think it means?"

"Let's talk later."

There stood Keith Wesley. "What's the big secret?"

I looked him straight in the eye. "It's just that Chief, a secret. Why are you here for the second time today?"

He handed Sandy his credit card. His focus stayed on me. "I bought a house. It was supposed to close on it today so I gave up my apartment. Now I'm homeless."

In no way did I try to keep the sarcasm out of my voice." What a shame, sleeping in your car are you?"

"No, I'm at Granny's Bed and Breakfast. I should be in my house in a few days."

As we talked, Nutmeg came from out of her hiding place and stood beside me. She emitted a long low growl. "I don't think she likes you, Keith." I turned to Sandra. "I'm going to the kitchen. Keep her with you, please."

He stepped in front of me. If I wanted to go any further, I would have to circle him. He reached over and took hold of my arm. His grip was not hard enough to hurt me or leave a mark. "Am I under arrest, Chief Wesley?

Nutmeg took a step toward him and bared her

teeth. He dropped my arm and took a step back. "Whoa, puppy."

The dog didn't stop. She took a protective step in front of me. "What's so important you have to touch me?"

He looked at me, glanced down to the dog, and to Sandra, who wanted him to sign his statement. "You're always in such a hurry to get away from me. I wanted to tell you something."

"Here I am. What do you want to tell me?"

He looked at the dog and then toward Sandra again. "It can wait.'

"Oh gee," I said, "I thought you might want to apologize again."

His face turned tomato red. He left without another word.

Sandra pushed a few buttons and the register did the rest. It spit out a printed report of all the revenue from the day. "What was that all about?"

"I'm going to lock the door. Everyone's gone. He scares and excites me. You know, they say good-looking men get by with more than ugly men,"

"Arizona, I don't like the way he touched you."

"Yeah, and then there's that," I said flatly.

Chapter Nineteen

Someone knocked on my apartment door at five a.m. Nutmeg got there first but didn't bark or growl. The number of people who could knock and not have to be buzzed into the foyer was limited to Mom, Sandy and James.

I opened it. There stood James. "You should go to the restaurant. Your mother's there, changing things."

I had on flannel sleep pants and an oversized tee shirt. I grabbed a sweatshirt. Slid into my slippers and followed him.

Nutmeg hung back a respectable distance but followed.

I could hear my mother barking orders. What I saw, I didn't expect. All of the line cooks, the servers on the breakfast shift and Lewis stood in a line against the wall away from her.

My assessment of the situation was, Mother

wanted something done and not one person moved a muscle to help her accomplish her goal, whatever it happened to be. Her focus stayed on the line of our employees in front of her.

I walked up within three inches of her and asked, "Mother, what are you doing?" She jumped, turned around, and yelled, "You're going to give me a heart attack. You do that too much. I think you're trying to kill me."

"I think it's a toss-up as to who causes who to have one first." I looked up at the crew. "Everyone go back to work. Emma is finished with you for the time being."

"Arizona, what gives you the right to order those people around?"

"Because they all work for me. They don't know to follow your lead. I'll get us a cup of coffee and a pastry. Find a seat. I'll be right back."

By the time I walked back into the dining room, she had taken all of the ketchup and mustard containers off the tables and sat them in the serving area. "Mother, please come sit down, we need to talk."

She finished putting them in rows of ten before she joined me. "Where's the cream and sugar?"

I looked around. "Maybe they are over there with the other condiments." After I retrieved them I sat down. "What's up? Why did you have everyone out here? Did you forget we open in half an hour and nothing is in its place?"

She looked around. "I wanted to clean the condiment containers, wipe out the sweetener trays and dust those plastic flowers on the tables you refuse to change. I've seen your living space. It's worse than when you were a child. I can't let my café become a pigsty."

"There are a multitude of questions I would like you to answer, but let's begin with the most important. The mustard, catsup, flowers, salt and pepper shakers, cream and sugar servers are clean. They are wiped down every night and emptied, washed, and refilled once a week. These are all things you taught me. Do you come down here because you're bored?"

"I come down because that silly will says I had to retire at seventy-five and I didn't and don't want to be put out to pasture."

"But Mom, that was five years ago. Would you like to have a job?"

"Well, yes, what did you have in mind, kitchen manager, server supervisor, menu consultant?"

"How about Senior Hostess? You can pick your hours, wear what you want, so long as you're completely dressed and you can pick the two days each week as your days off."

"What does it pay?"

I was flabbergasted. "What does it pay? Mother, every Friday a deposit is made into your account at Moonstone Savings. Do you ever check it?"

"No, but whatever you intend to pay me, I want a raise."

"We'll talk about it later. Most people go to work first before they ask for a raise. When will you work your first shift?"

"I'll let you know, Arizona. Meanwhile, you had better go. Customers are arriving and you don't have the tables set properly."

I stared at her and shook my head as she left.

I knew the day couldn't get much worse. People were inside; no one stood in front to seat them. I needed to put the condiments where they belonged. I took a deep breath.

As I scooted my chair away from the table to stand, Chief Wesley waved the ring in front of my eyes.

I grabbed for it. "Where did you get that?"

He raised his arm to put the evidence out of my reach. "A better question is where did you get it?"

I moved both hands to my hips and stomped my foot. "You answer my question and I'll answer yours." The only two times I had been angry all month included Keith Wesley.

He brought the ring back to eye level and wiped it on his shirt. "Your mother gave it to me."

"How can that be? When I got up she was down here causing trouble. Before that, the ring was in my desk drawer."

He stepped closer. "So you admit you withheld evidence?"

I went for the gold band again. He dropped it into his shirt pocket. "I didn't withhold anything. Nutmeg found it on the lake shore. I didn't know what it was until last night."

"A judge has a search warrant in front of him. Once he signs it and Randy gets it here, we will look through your apartment to see if you have any other important little trinkets up there."

Two thoughts flashed through my mind. I would strangle my mother next time I saw her and Keith

Wesley and Randy Malone, and no telling who else would look at everything I owned. Unfortunately, most of it lay on the floor or on top of the furniture.

I wanted to fall through the floor.

Breakfast hours kept the entire staff hopping. We sat in the kitchen to wait for Officer Malone. Two hours passed and still no warrant. Keith's phone rang and he stepped outside to answer it. He disconnected a phone call as he came back to the counter. "We aren't going to make that search today."

"Gee, Keith, did you get your toes stepped on? Seems as though each and every time I see you, your face turns another shade of red."

I saw him swallow his words. It did my heart good.

Once he left, I tried to figure out how my mother got into my home without me realizing it. Nutmeg wouldn't bark or growl at her.

It had to be the night before while I took a shower.

Before I tried to put the morning behind me, I made one more call. "Is this Davis Lock and Key Service? Please come to Moonstone Lake Café' I need new locks on my apartment. If you come here and ask for Arizona, I'll go with you and show you what I want."

What I really wanted was to electrify the door so if anyone touched it.

Zap.

Chapter Twenty

I forfeited my morning jog to pay a visit to Dr. Stone. I hadn't seen him since Chief Chase's going away party. I hoped our old relationship slid right into a new partnership with Chief Wesley. The difference being, I had no intention of ever telling Keith about my visit.

The office door stood open. I poked my head around the corner to make sure nothing unsavory went on inside. My luck, Keith sat on one side, Dr. Stone on the other. They studied a report. "I'm not sure what the substance is. It's nothing I've come across before. Her body tells me she was in the water for at least forty-eight hours. There was so little of it I can't really say she died from poisoning or drowning.

"She had an enlarged heart and small lungs from the bulk she carried. I'm not convinced she didn't get scared and die of a heart attack before she hit the water. I'm sorry Chief Wesley, this one has me stumped. I've never seen anything like it and I've been at this for forty years. I sent a blood sample to the state lab and requested a tox screen. It should be back within ten days.

"Meanwhile you know it had to be someone who could put her in the boat. If she was already in the boat they needed the strength to push two hundred and fifty pounds of dead weight into the water."

I heard Keith's voice. "So I'm looking for a man strong enough to be able to move her. We found her wedding ring on the beach. Not close to the shore or the boat. This gets more confusing by the day. Thanks for your time. Let me know when you get your report from the state."

His chair scraped across the concrete floor and I ran out. Nutmeg sat by the entrance. We hid around the corner of the building and watched Keith leave.

Nutmeg let out a low growl. I said no and she didn't make another sound.

We remained hidden for ten minutes. I knew he would have moved on by then. I thought about their conversation all the way home.

Heart attack, poison, fear, but she definitely didn't drown.

The next three days it rained. Rain didn't usually slow down business but it rained hard enough to leave puddles on flat ground.

I cleaned my apartment, all of it. It took hour upon hour. I never put clothes in the closet. On the rare occasions I cleaned it up I swore I would keep it like that. My pledge this time lasted an entire week.

I didn't have to buy clothes. Some of them had

been on the floor so long I forgot I had them. It was a cheap way to get new clothes. I sat on a bed and thought how sordid my joke was and how lucky I was Mother didn't have my place condemned after she saw it.

I decided not to say anything about the ring. Next time she tried to get into my space, she would realize I knew.

Our problem stemmed from a hundred-plus-year-old will. It made the elder female of the family leave the business before some were ready to go.

Well, that wasn't exactly true. My grandmother left two days after Mom took over, went on a cruise around the world, came back three years later with a husband, a smile on her face, and bought a huge house on the north side of the lake.

Every morning she went for a swim until she was well into her late eighties.

They found her dead at ninety-four in a lounge chair by the swimming pool with a martini, and a book titled Sex for Seniors.

Mother was nothing like Grandma.

Having a clean apartment made me happy. I told myself it would make me more productive.

After I scrubbed my tub, I filled it with bubble bath and salts for a good soak. I went so far as to put several candles around and turn the lights low before I climbed in.

Nutmeg laid on the floor with her back to me. Did she do it to give me privacy?

I slid into the water as far as I could, laid back, and closed my eyes.

Bong!

A computer went off in my head. I jumped out of the tub, slipped on the wet floor on my way into the other room to get a pen and paper.

I wrote down the thought I had, put the now wet tablet on the floor next to me, laid back down in the hot water and closed my eyes once again.

Ruth's Obituary. I picked up my pen and paper and wrote it down.

Rest...Relax...

Name of the foundation, scribbled it on my note pad

Relax...Closed my eyes

Did anyone steal from the foundation? Wrote down; find name of Ruth's charity and read about it.

Nutmeg stood, turned around to face me, she followed my acrobatics with her eyes.

Relax...

Run a check on Mark O'Shay. I read my entire list and decided it was complete.

Once more I sunk low into the tub, closed my eyes and tried to relax.

The water was cold.

I toweled off, put on some sweat clothes and prepared to take Nutmeg for her walk.

We had only taken two steps off the front stoop when the dog's hair bristled. She pawed the ground and bared her teeth. "Who's there?"

Chief Keith Wesley stepped out of the shadows. "It's me."

"Keith, should I be afraid of you?"

"Of course not, Arizona, I'm the police."

I pulled Nutmeg back. She kept her nose within an inch of his knee. "You were at the restaurant twice yesterday. You had a ring from my private apartment. Now you are standing in front of me. It isn't comforting."

"I told you I had a room at Granny's Bed and Breakfast. The buildings are one in the same. The only thing between me and you is a firewall."

"Trust me," I said. "It's not the only thing." I turned around and began to walk the other way. "Excuse us. It's late. Nutmeg needs her walk and I need my sleep."

"May I walk with you?"

"I can't keep you from it. It's a public sidewalk."

Nutmeg wanted to run so I undid her leash and off she went.

"Do you walk by yourself every night?" he asked.

"I'm not alone. Nutmeg is with me."

He looked in every direction. "She's not here now."

"Keith, Chief Wesley, you are scaring me."

He took a step closer to me. Our hips brushed lightly as we walked. "You can call me Keith."

Nutmeg came out of nowhere, jumped on Keith with both legs and pushed him back two steps with her paws. She turned around and placed herself between the Chief and me. I reached down to Nutmeg. "See, I'm not alone."

"That dog isn't normal."

"I know, isn't she great?"

"Listen, Arizona, I didn't mean anything. I saw you and thought we could take a walk together. We got off on the wrong foot. I'd like to change that."

"I'm not the one who set the tone for this relationship. You called me in and laid down the law according to Keith Wesley. You had no idea who or what I am."

He turned to face me, Nutmeg made a low unfriendly sound. Wesley stepped back. "Can't we try to be friends?"

"Maybe another time." We were back in front of the porch. "In the daylight."

Nutmeg and I went inside. I locked the door behind me.

I glanced back to the sidewalk. Keith stood still and stared my way.

Uhm...

I wanted to start my investigation but since I cleaned my entire apartment in one evening, didn't relax in the tub as I had intended, and topped off my night with an inexplicable meeting with the chief. I decided to wait. We went to bed instead.

The next morning, Nutmeg and I had an eventful run. Carol Sparks, the owner of Bueno Taco Shop, lay in the middle of the path holding her ankle. Nutmeg went up to her and licked her face. From the look she gave me, I'd have to guess she didn't like it.

I knelt down. "My goodness, Carol, are you hurt? I guess that's a silly question. Where are you hurt?"

She lay down and straightened out one leg. It didn't take a doctor to know her other leg had a fracture.

"My leg is broken. I can tell by looking. When I fell, I put my hands out in front of me. My left wrist is a mess. The right one doesn't burn that bad so it might be okay."

I took the phone out of my pocket and dialed 911. Within five minutes, Fire and Rescue pulled up in a fire truck, followed by an ambulance from Mercy Hospital, and of course, Chief Wesley.

I wondered if he had any other deputies besides Randy. Moonstone Lake had twenty-two hundred residents. I would think they would need more than two. They had to sleep sometime.

While the paramedics worked to stabilize Carol's leg, I walked to her taco shop to tell her husband the news. The first step I took put me face to face with Keith. He smelled like lemon. "We've got to quit meeting like this." I smiled as I said it, but he made me nervous. He always stood one step too close.

"Miss Summers. It's nice to see you this morning." He reached down to pat Nutmeg on top of the head. The dog let him know she didn't like it. "Do you have a minute?"

I looked at my phone to check the time. I had plenty. "Sorry, I'll have to hurry as it is."

"Could I take you to dinner? We could go somewhere on the north side where you don't have to cook."

"Honestly, my week is full. I would like to come to your office. I have something for you to look into."

He smiled. Geez, he rivaled a TV star. When he smiled, two dimples appeared in his cheeks. I wished I hadn't seen that. "When would you like to come?"

"Unfortunately it will have to be after seven. I work tonight."

He smiled again. "How about we meet at Danny's Bar? It's warm enough, the garden will be open."

"Keith. This is not a social call. It's about the Freedman murder. I have something to tell you."

He stepped aside. "I'll see you at the station about

seven-thirty then."

Carl Sparks, Carol's husband, and co-owner met me part way. "Tell me all those sirens and flashing lights aren't for my wife."

"They are but don't panic. She tripped over her shoelace and fell. Her leg is obviously broken and it is iffy about her wrist. You might as well head back to the shop. They said there was no need for you to come to the hospital right now. They have to examine her and take x-rays."

"You know, Ary, I tried and tried to get her to walk and not jog, I even read her an article about how it might be healthier for someone her age to walk."

I went back with him to the taco shop. The smell of seasoned meat, hot peppers, and baking taco shells greeted us three doors away. "Do you have enough help without Carol, and you, when you leave for the hospital?"

"No, not really, I have one out sick. I had to fire one and I have two off today. This isn't one of our busy days."

"It's not one of our busy times either. I'll send a server and a line cook. Serving is pretty much the same everywhere. Tell David how you want things cooked. He cooks Mexican for us. It won't be like yours but he is a good guy and a quick study. Keep them for a few days. I have two coming in today so we have some backup."

I thought he might cry. Carol and Carl were older. I didn't know how much older, I never could judge age. They didn't open Bueno Taco until they both retired from their chosen profession. They had moved from California to Missouri. I didn't know much about them."

Nutmeg and I ran back to the apartment. I showered quickly and went down to work.

CHAPTER TWENTY-ONE

Mixed emotions and thoughts played ping pong in my brain and stomach at the thought of the meeting with Keith. The conversation we had the first day made it clear he wanted me to stay out of police business. I didn't.

After I showered, dressed, put my makeup on and combed my hair, I didn't look in the mirror the rest of the day. A self-help book would have most likely said I had something wrong with me.

The truth…when I left the house in the morning, I looked as good as I was able to look with the assets I had. If I didn't catch my reflection in a mirror or a window, I had the same notion all day. One look and my confidence sunk, my hair looked tangled, lips chapped, skirt wrinkled, eye liner smudged, and my mascara resembled raccoon eyes.

I wanted to look good at the police station. I went upstairs, brushed my teeth and unruly hair, tied it back with a scrunchy, reapplied my make up, and headed out.

On the way down the stairs, I ran into Sandra. She climbed as I descended. "Wow, you look fantastic. Do you have a date?"

"Yes, with Nutmeg.

"Come on Ary, fess-up. Is it Randy or Keith?"

"It's Keith, but it isn't what you think. I have a clue and I want him to look into it. I can't just walk in there like I did with Chief Chase and get the information I need."

She looked me over again. "All I can say is; he can't say no to you the once he sees the way you look. Bat your eyes and you're in."

I didn't bother to answer. Nutmeg and I bounded down the stairs.

Sandy looked over the railing at the top of the staircase. "If it isn't too late, stop and tell me all about it when you get home."

I yelled back. "You mean if I get back before nine?"

I couldn't have ordered a more superb evening. The shops were closed. The tourist season was over a month away. The lights from their signs reflected back from the calm water. We took our time and enjoyed the solitude. I walked more slowly because I dreaded Keith Wesley's reaction to the subject of my visit.

It seemed like only a minute before I stood at the front door. I took a deep breath and went in. I took Nutmeg with me.

Chief Keith Wesley met me at the door. "Hi, would you mind leaving the dog outside?"

"You mean, Nutmeg? Yes, I would."

His face clouded over but he didn't say anything. "Let's go into my office. I took the liberty of getting you a diet Dr. Pepper. I know you like them."

Geez, this is too much zipped through my mind. "Thanks," came out my mouth.

He even had a glass with ice.

Once we got settled, he asked, "What's this about?"

"A man named Mark O'Shay."

He leaned toward his desk and rested his forearms on it with his arms crossed and his hands tucked under his elbows. I had seen it done a million times when someone stood, but never while seated. "Who's Mark O'Shay?"

I crossed my legs and tried to relax. "Mark O'Shay is the best man at Dillon Freedman and Stacy Young's wedding next Saturday night."

"And I care about this, why?"

"If you investigate him you'll find out he and Ruth Freedman had a history. They detested one another since Dillon and Mark were children. He once tripped her on purpose. She fell and broke her nose. One of the many circumstances about the wedding Mrs. Freedman was upset and angry over."

He stood, walked around the desk, and sat on the top of it, our knees touched. Nutmeg moved from her spot next to me and lay down between the Chief's legs and mine. "Arizona, how do you know that? I have never even heard of anyone named Mark O'Shay!"

I leaned away from him. "As I told you before when you were yelling at me, you know when we first met. I have sources, I know people, and I overhear things."

"Who told you about Mark?"

"Chief, I can't tell you that. If word got out and people found out I didn't keep a confidence, I'd be finished as a go-to person."

"Ary, you don't care if I call you Ary, do you? What is a go-to person?"

"Obviously you don't know because you've never been one. It's a person you can always talk to in confidence, tell anything to, and your name stays out of it."

He walked back around the desk, sat down and took a yellow legal pad out of his desk drawer. "Interesting. Tell me all you know about Mark O'Shay and why he could be our killer."

"This is what I know. You'll have to research the rest. When Paul Chase ran this station, I went to the files, used the computers, and resources, and did the work myself."

"We're not there yet."

"Okay, He's twenty-five years old. As I said, he and Ruth had a horrible relationship from the beginning. Mark has a degree in business management. He's a stockbroker at Martin and Hanes, in New York.

"He has been married once. His ex-wife took an ex parte against him, and before the divorce, the police were at the house for more than one domestic abuse complaint.

"The rest you need to find out yourself. I would like to know what you find. If he didn't kill her, I'd like to move on down my list."

He stood. "You'll be the first to know."

I looked him straight in the eye. "Was that a sarcastic remark?"

Keith leaned over and put his hands palms down on the desk with his elbows straight. "It was not sarcastic. I should never have jumped down your throat when I met you. Will you ever let that go?"

"I'm not sure."

He walked around and put his tablet back in the drawer. "Let me drive you and Nutmeg home. I know you could get there on your own, but I'm going there anyway."

Keith and I rode in the front. Nutmeg sat in the back. When we drove up in front of the four-plex, he asked, "will you tell me who else is on your list?"

"If you clear Mark O'Shay, I'll give you the next name."

"You are remarkably observant, everybody's friend, and you might be of help after all."

I opened the door to the police cruiser and got out. "Thank you, I think."

CHAPTER TWENTY-TWO

Preparations for Stacy and Dillon's wedding took up any spare time I might have had the next week. The Young's had rented the banquet room. If no event was scheduled in the room we used it for overflow.

The cleaning crew arrived on Thursday morning and by evening the room shined.

A rental company on the north side of the lake brought the table cloths, silverware, and chafing dishes. We had found out years before, we saved money if we rented the silver services rather than clean, polish, and store them. It also gave us a better choice of items. The chefs went through the menu and noted what piece would best serve it.

Saturday morning, Michael and Dottie, from the bakery, and Sherri from the flower shop all buzzed around the room. At noon they came to the kitchen to ask James, Lewis, and I to take a last look before the bridal party arrived.

The instant we stepped out of the kitchen I got a whiff of flowers. The closer I got, the more I realized I had never smelled anything like it. An intoxicating, sweet exotic gardenia-like smell radiated through the room. "What kind of flowers are those?"

Sherry walked to the nearest table and gently pulled one of the white long-stemmed beauties out of a vase where it was tucked in with pink, white, and magenta daisies. "They are tuberoses. Aren't they divine?"

Dottie stepped closer to smell it. "Is it a bulb? Could I grow it here?"

Michael leaned in to get a better look at it. "We had better leave that conversation for another day. I would guess Sherri would rather you didn't grow your own. I would certainly prefer no one baked their own cakes.''

Everyone laughed.

James and Lewis went to the serving line to make sure it met their standards. "This is a beautiful setup. We'll put the salad first, then the roasted potatoes, followed by candied carrots. Lewis will be with me all night since Michael is responsible for the cake and cupcakes." I stated.

Michael stepped up. "I did tell you that Dottie and I will serve the cakes."

Lewis and James nodded yes. I asked, "Tell us if it is set up the way you like it. Move things around if you need to."

"If you want any help with that let me know," Lewis said.

Off to the side, on a smaller table sat the groom's armadillo cake. Michael saw me staring at it and said.

"I am proud of myself for that cake. I had to rely on the internet for a close-up picture so I could put on the details."

I asked the chefs if they wanted people in certain places while we were serving. Lewis went over to one of the tables. "We should put a warm basket of bread and the butter on the tables an hour before they get here. I should think the iced tea glasses and water glasses should be filled. We can either designate two servers to keep them full or put a pitcher of each on the tables."

Michael looked at his cake display. "Congratulations everyone, it is fantastic. They only wanted a presentation cake. I have 300 cupcakes, one-fifty chocolate, and the same in vanilla. Should we let them file through to get the cake or serve it?"

I began to roam around the room. "I'm for the line. It'll keep them occupied while we transition the dining room into a dance floor. We'll close the café at six. We should have more than enough time to move tables and chairs. The DJ will handle his own equipment."

I stood against the wall to take a break and a deep breath when Keith walked in. "What are you doing here?"

He came into the room and turned in a circle. "This is fabulous. What is the smell? Would you believe I was invited?"

"No, No, I wouldn't. I assume those are rhetorical questions since you didn't give me time to answer. Why don't you move along? I have a long night ahead and I need to keep my head in the game."

The Chief stood in front of me. "So you're saying

you can't concentrate while I'm around?"

I went around him and into the kitchen to go over things with the staff one more time. I didn't have time to babysit or spar with him. Secretly, I wouldn't have minded talking to him.

I had rented white shirts and red bow ties from a uniform provider. Each server was responsible for his or her own black slacks and shoes.

We did three to four weddings a year, but it only took a good waiter or waitress a few minutes to get the hang of things.

Keith followed me. "I'm not here to disrupt. I'll stay completely out of sight. I need to see how the wedding party interacts with one another and get a look at Mark O'Shay. You might be on to something there."

"Fine, but don't get in anyone's way. It's not like I can call the police and have you removed."

I heard, *ouch*, as I left the room. I turned around. "By the way, this is a formal affair. When you come back, I expect you to be in a coat and tie."

Stacy, Dillon, Jackson and Denise Young seemed to have a festive time, Roger Freedman, not so much. I thought he might be sad because Ruth wasn't there. His mood could have been guilt.

The wedding took place at noon. After pictures and a ride around the lake in a limo, the wedding party arrived at five. We had all three courses served, bussed, and coffee served by seven.

Dillon stood and tapped his glass with a spoon. "I'd like to share with you the history of the Armadillo cake. When Mark and I were nine we were in awe of armadillos, and hated it when one got run over.

"We thought the answer was an armadillo crossing. We made two signs, *Be Watchful* and the other said, *Armadillo Crossing*. We faced one north and the one south on the main highway.

"There were as many dead animals after we placed the signs as before. The local television station and newspaper picked it up as a human interest story.

"If that wasn't bad enough, the national news aired it too. We became the laughing stocks of our neighborhood. We had no idea that when an armadillo got frightened, it jumped straight up. No one ran over them, they hit the underneath of the car and killed themselves.

"Mark and I became known as the Armadillo Boys. The name stayed with us through high school."

The entire room broke out in laughter.

We opened the dining room and the party began.

Keith arrived after dinner. He roamed around the room and chatted with some of the guests. I noticed two things about him. He stayed away from the wedding party and he looked gorgeous in a pink shirt, maroon and grey striped tie, a dark maroon sport coat and grey slacks that hugged his muscular legs.

The last guest left at midnight.

CHAPTER TWENTY-THREE

I fell into the chair behind me, closed my eyes and stretched. Nutmeg came and put both of her paws in my lap. "I bet you're tired of staying away from the people, aren't you pretty girl?" I opened my eyes and there sat Keith. "Geez, are you still here?"

"Yes. Did you notice no one made mention of Ruth Freedman, not her husband, or her son, nobody? Isn't that strange?"

I stood and stretched. "I was a little too busy to observe anything but empty glasses and junk on the floor someone could trip over. But you're right. I would have thought her son would have given a toast or said something when he danced with Denise Young for the mother and son dance"

"Well then, it is a good thing I stayed around,"

Nutmeg went toward the hallway that led to the four-plex. "I'll say goodnight now. Tomorrow's Sunday. Brunch starts at eleven and I need to be there. It'll be a short night and I'm tired."

I found it amusing, if he took a step closer than the dog thought he should, she immediately stepped in front of him. "When do you think you'll have time to discuss Mark O'Shay with me?"

"Wow, you've done a complete one-eighty. First, you didn't want me around and now you want to collaborate on the case? I think if I'm still alert after tomorrow's lunch I could find time."

"I hoped we could talk now."

"Actually Keith, I'm too tired to think, I'm going to bed"

I didn't have to be a detective to figure out he was either angry or hurt. I didn't know him well enough to know which.

His eyes narrowed. He bent his head down, pursed his lips, took a deep breath and looked at me. "I do understand. It can wait until tomorrow." He headed for the door. "I can solve this mystery without you. Since you seemed to be such a sleuth, I thought you would want to be in on the capture."

"I do. Tomorrow afternoon you'll have my full attention."

He took giant steps toward the front door and tried to yank it open. The deadbolt had been locked and he nearly pulled his arm out of the socket.

I thought it best to ignore his mishap. I unlocked the door, smiled and said, goodnight in my sweetest voice. As he walked out the door he mumbled something under his breath. I thought it better not to have him repeat it. I locked the door behind him and went back down the hall to go home. On a whim instead of going up, I went to the front door and looked out.

He wasn't there.

I opened the door to a storybook day. The sun shined down from a cloudless sky. I smelled spring in the air. I took a blanket and laid it at the water's edge for a nap. Nutmeg served as my pillow.

"Since we spoke last, I did more research on Mark O'Shay. The true story is nothing like the records portray. He married a girl he got pregnant in high school. She took drugs, stole a car, and did all sorts of unsavory criminal acts. Her father was a district attorney. The cases were turned around to make Mark look guilty."

"Nice to see you Keith, take a deep breath and have a seat." I turned over on my side to face him. Nutmeg didn't move. I could only assume she didn't think the chief a threat at the present time. I yawned. "Seems far-fetched, it would be a huge cover-up. It would include patrolmen, judges, court reporters, newspapers, and people on the street. It seems totally implausible."

Keith sat next to me and tossed rocks into the water. "Her dad was a powerful man. He ran for governor, but ended up in jail for fraud. I think he's still there. Mark divorced the girl, moved to New York City and never looked back."

"That's all fascinating, Chief, but what does it have to do with the murder of Ruth Freedman?"

He looked back at me. "Mark O'Shay left Moonstone Lake on Sunday morning before they all came to your place for Sunday Brunch. The doorman said he came home at seven-thirty, ordered a pizza, and never left the building."

"Denise said Dillon and Stacy took him to the airport and barely got back in time to go to the buffet. It sounds like everyone is telling the truth. The big question is what difference does it make? Do you think he's a suspect? To come back he would have to sneak out and fly back to Moonstone Lake, kill her and fly home. I can't see it happening."

"You're right. I was thinking out loud."

Nutmeg began to stir and I sat up. "Sure you were. But it does take one more name off the list. We're down to Stacy and Dillon, Mr. and Mrs. Young and Mr. Freedman."

"I know Stacy Young and Dillon Freedman didn't kill her."

"Arizona, I can't just take your word for it. I'll have to investigate."

Nutmeg stood and shook. "I have a source. Leave Stacy, Dillon, and Mrs. Young off your suspect list. I can't tell you how I know until we solve the case."

"I need to go… I can't remember when we were so busy on a Sunday. I need some sleep.

He reached down and gave me a hand up. Nutmeg didn't like it. She sat next to me and made a low grrrrr the entire time.

I laid my head down at eight-thirty. The last time I went to bed so early I had strep throat.

Someone woke me out of my sound sleep by pounding on the door. Again, when Nutmeg didn't bark or get alarmed. It could only be one of three people. I slept in a pair of shorts and an oversized tee shirt so I opened the door without a robe.

There stood Mother and Aunt Sandra.

Mother pushed past me and went to the living

room. Sandra shrugged her shoulders and followed.

The clock flashed 6 a.m.

I stood by the window between the couch Sandra occupied and the chair Mother sat in with her arms crossed like a petulant child.

"It doesn't look as if anyone died, got maimed, or needs an ambulance, so why are we having this little coffee clutch so early in the morning?"

Sandy prodded Mom. "Tell her Emma."

"I need ten thousand dollars."

I couldn't hide my surprise. "Geez Mom, that's a goodly sum. Why do you need it?"

"I want to loan it to Bill Tanner."

"You mean the same Bill Tanner who lives in his car behind The Grab and Go?"

"Yes."

"Maybe I should sit down," I said. "One of you tell me what's going on. Last I heard Mother, you'd sworn off men, said you would never trust one again. Bill is a man, who's dirty, homeless, and spends a few nights a month in jail for drunk and disorderly conduct."

"Arizona, you should never judge people. If I've told you that once, I've told you a million times."

Mother was the reason I chose never to marry and have children. I looked at Aunt Sandra. "You're awfully quiet. You know what this is all about or you'd be home in bed."

She took a deep breath. No doubt in my mind she didn't want to be in my living room at six a.m. with Mother and one of her schemes.

"According to Emma, Bill won the Irish Sweepstakes. The prize is twelve million dollars. For him to redeem the ticket he has to send ten thousand dollars to Dublin."

"I've heard that one before. Mother, why do you want to loan it to him? Isn't there someone else who could step up?"

"Sit down, Arizona. You look like a vulture looming over me with those boney arms and legs. He put money down on the old Jameson house on Rosewood Cove Drive."

I sat. "If he needs ten thousand dollars to get his lottery winnings, how did he put money down on a house? Especially, that house. It's the biggest one on the lake. If he put five percent down it would be well over a hundred thousand dollars."

"He didn't actually put the money down yet. He will, when the money arrives from overseas. It has nine bedrooms"

"Mother, what would Bill Tanner do with a nine-bedroom house?"

Sandy went into the kitchen and in a minute I heard the coffee pot making its noises and the bold smell of freshly brewed coffee.

Mom sat forward on the couch, her butt barely clipped the cushion and it's no small fanny. "He's going to help all of his friends who are down and out. Sara, Darrell, Max, Speedy, and Runt will live there. I thought I might have a room over there so I could cook for them. You know how I love to cook."

Aunt Sandra came in with three cups of coffee, each one fixed the way we liked it. Mom relaxed some, took a sip of coffee, and sat the cup on the table next to her.

My aunt sat back in the rocker and joined in the

conversation. "The people you named don't have five dollars between them. If you want to cook, you could cook at your own restaurant. Heaven knows the line cooks would love the help."

I stood, walked over, and sat beside my mom. "The bottom line is you want the money so you can loan Bill enough to get his winnings so there will be money for a down payment on a house for you to move into with a bunch of people we have been feeding with leftovers from the restaurant for the last two years?"

She looked at me as if I had just murdered her cat. "All people are created equal, Arizona. It could be us out there on the street. This is nothing but a loan against my portion of the restaurant. So what's your answer?"

"Simply. No."

"But I earned the money."

"You are a smart lady, Mother. Think about it. If you won the lottery, what would you do? You would drive to the lottery office and claim your winnings."

"But my dear daughter, this is Ireland. The money is for the rate of exchange Bill will have to claim the money. I'll get it all back."

I put my hand on her arm. She was having no part of that. She jerked away and nearly knocked her coffee cup off the table and onto the floor.

Her sister lowered her voice and spoke in a loving tone. "Emma, it isn't on the up and up. I bet I can find this same scam on the internet and read it to you. The thing I want to know is why do you want to move in with him and all of those people?"

"I really don't. I was at the park a few weeks ago

and Bill told me about the lottery. One by one, over the last few weeks, the others began to come by and talk to me. They would tell me how I could change everyone's life with a few dollars which would be a pittance compared to what I have.

"Bill said we could all live at the big house, play cards, and have fun. I haven't ever had time for fun. I'm ready now."

For the first time in years, I hugged my mom, and she let me. "This is a scam Mom. Once they get the money, there will be a reason the Irish ticket didn't win. I'm sorry you are lonesome. You haven't been to work, one day since I offered you a job."

She stood, tears in her eyes. "That wasn't a job. It was to appease me so I would leave you alone. You know I can't withdraw the money without your signature. I hate being under your thumb."

Nutmeg went over, sat at her feet, and raised her hand to shake Mom's.

Mother tried not to smile, but she did. "Arizona, I see your point, but I can't face those people and tell them my daughter wouldn't give me the money. It would be humiliating."

"I'll take care of it. Don't worry. I will never tell them it takes your signature and mine to get money out of the Café Account."

"Thank you, Arizona. In my heart, I felt funny about the entire thing and to tell you the truth, I'm not sure Bill bathes regularly."

"Go back to bed now. Don't worry about a thing. There's a cruise all the way from one end of the Mississippi River to the other. Lots of seniors are going. There are only a few cabins left. Why don't we talk about it later today? I bet Martha Adams would like to go."

I couldn't go back to sleep. I needed to think. If I didn't watch out, I would be in the same predicament as Mother. In two weeks I'd be thirty-two years old. There were no romantic interests standing in the wings. I couldn't see having a child in my forties. I also couldn't see getting pregnant just to have someone to take over the business. I certainly didn't intend to adopt a child so I'd have an heir.

The more I thought, I realized cooking, running the restaurant, and solving crimes were all I knew. Of the three of them, I liked crime fighting best.

I didn't know what I would do with a child if I had one. They took time, money, love, and affection.

An attorney came to the group home where I lived and told me I'd been adopted. I was to move to Missouri with a nice lady who happened to be waiting in the office. It was the day before my fifth birthday.

I know Mom had to fly to Arizona to pick me up and escort me home. I'm guessing my real mom named me Arizona, not very inventive on her part. I think my last name was Jones.

I don't think Mom has left Missouri since. With all the children in the world who wanted a forever home, I was perplexed as to why Emma picked a certain five year old from so far away. There was a reason, but I didn't know what it was. One day I would seek out the truth, but not now. The mention of my adoption sent Mom into a panic. I was certain Aunt Sandy knew my story, but she wouldn't speak of it either.

Nearly six weeks had passed and we were no closer than before as to who killed Ruth Freedman. I got dressed and Nutmeg and I went for a run. The pink and orange of the sky reflected off the surface of the water. Awe inspiring, sunsets and sunrises fascinated me. I had watched the sun rise for years. Everyone was different but equally sublime.

I was so focused on the water, I ran over Nutmeg. One foot kicked her and with the other I stepped on her. She yelped so loud, other runners stopped to look at us. A guy I hadn't noticed walked up and asked if she was okay.

Nutmeg went wild. She barked and snarled until I had to put my hand under her collar to hold her back.

Needless to say, he made a hasty exit. I knew I'd seen him before, but I didn't recognize his voice. He wore a knit cap pulled down past his eyebrows. The running gear he wore consisted of a black Under Armor turtleneck stretch shirt, black tights, and nondescript New Balance tennis shoes, none of which I recognized.

I didn't spend much time on who it might be because of Nutmeg. I wanted to find out if I injured her or she had no use for men dressed in black.

My dog had pawed up another ring. I looked toward the lake to get my bearings. We were at the edge of the rental docks. Several John boats remained loosely tied along the west side. They didn't log who took them. They belonged to the City of Moonstone Lake and the summer folk, mostly the kids rowed them around. Unless someone saw the killer take a boat, there was no way to track him.

My cell phone beeped, it was Keith. "You'll never

guess who's moving to Moonstone Lake?"

"Roger Freedman."

His voice dropped. "How did you know?"

"Come on, Chief. Who else would move to the lake that I would care about? And, I think I just saw him while I was running this morning,"

"Are you out running now?"

"Yes. Nutmeg found another ring. I don't know what it signifies, and next to it was a black leather glove. Strange we never noticed it before. I take that back. The area from the path to the water's edge has been tasseled."

"Tasseled? Like an exotic dancer?"

I ignored him. "Maybe that's why the ring is on top. I need to go. Later gater."

I went to work and took the ring with me. I intended to keep track of the new find. I wouldn't put it anywhere someone else could pick it up.

I didn't have to work on Monday night. The way people ate on Sunday, they were too full to come back so soon. Aunt Sandra had taken the day off to go to the outlet mall.

I was cashier or hostess if I wanted to be. Otherwise, I wandered around, talked to the few diners who came in and hung out in the kitchen with James. The chefs took turns taking a Monday night off.

"James, got a minute?"

He walked over to me. "Want something special for dinner?"

"Not now. I found another ring this morning, near the lake. Can you clean it for me?"

In no time, he came back with the ring in the palm

of his hand. "You say you got this off the ground near the lake?"

He handed me the now shiny piece of jewelry. "It's a chef's ring. Not exactly a chef's ring, but whoever owned it had to take a number of classes and learned difficult techniques to earn it."

"Do you and Lewis have a ring like this?"

James looked down at his hands. "I got one when I got my certificate. My fingers were not fat like they are now. It's in my apartment."

I turned around and ran smack into Keith. "Hi, if you want to give me the ring, I'll send it to the crime lab for cleaning."

James began to say something. I stopped him. "Have you had supper?"

"No, this is the first time I've stopped all day. Some homeless guy is panhandling all over the town. When I caught up with him, he said he won the Irish Lottery and needed money to claim it. I tried to explain to him it didn't work that way. He wouldn't listen."

I let it go. No use telling him about Mom. "Do you like shrimp?"

He nodded.

"James is the offer for dinner still open. If so, would you fix two shrimp scampi dinners? We'll be in my booth."

Keith asked, "Can you get any dinner you want at any time?"

"Sometimes, Mondays are slow. Listen, about your crime lab. Have you had to use it yet? It's slow. Here's the ring." I dropped it in his hand."

"Hum. Looks like a signet ring of some sort."

We stopped talking while our food was served. "What would you like to drink?"

"Iced tea."

"Make that two. Thanks, Benny."

"James says it belonged to a chef, gourmet cook, or food instructor. The symbol you can hardly make out is crossed knives and a toque."

"That's great Arizona, but I doubt it has anything to do with our murder."

"Don't be so sure."

I looked at the clock above the wait station. "We close in half an hour. I want to go upstairs and research our murder victim."

"Let's go to the station. We have Codes, and several other databases you can't access from here. But you know that, don't you?"

I smiled. "Okay. But not without Nutmeg."

We drove down the street in front of the Boardwalk. I'd been in a car more since Keith came to town than I had in years.

Nutmeg got rowdy in the back seat. She barked, whined and scratched the door latches. If Keith hadn't opened the window, I'm not sure she wouldn't have tried to chew her way out of the vehicle.

She ran at breakneck speed, stopped in front of the Ring the Bell Arcade, and hunched down as if she had been trained to crawl. The door opened, someone walked out and Nutmeg jumped on him so hard he fell on his back. She put her mouth on top of the guy's neck and stayed there until Keith and I caught up.

A gun laid four feet from the robber, open cloth bags of quarters were strewn everywhere. Keith looked my way. "Call her off, Ary."

Back up arrived and as they cleaned up the scene and waited for John Haywood, the owner, we took the man to jail.

He was none too happy to find out he had to share the backseat with the dog. The thief couldn't have gotten closer to the other side of the car if he tried.

Once we were in the office with the door closed Keith said, "It's difficult to believe someone dumped that dog. She's amazing."

Nutmeg answered for herself. " Arf, Arf."

"We found out Ruth Freedman had one foot in jail, had she not been thrown in the lake, most likely she would have been serving twenty-five to life in a New York state prison. She ran a family organization her father ran before her, The Martin Erb Foundation. Over two million dollars were unaccounted for. She would have been brought before the Grand Jury had she made it home."

Did she take the easy way out. I wondered."

"Well, Super Cop, I need to call it a night. Are you still rooming at Granny's? If not, Nutmeg and I can walk home."

"Yes, I'm at Granny's. I'm not the consummate home buyer. The house had several things wrong with it. Right now we are waiting for a window from Chicago. After what happened tonight, are you sure it's safe to walk?"

Nutmeg jumped up and barked.

"I swear she can understand everything we say."

I stood. "Don't forget it. If we don't walk now, we'll go out again when we get there. If you weren't super cop, you could go with us,"

He gave me a strange look. I had no idea what he had on his mind. He keyed the radio on the shoulder of his uniform. "Davis, Malone, where are you?"

"Malone here, we are 10-7 at Grab 'n Go."

"10-4, near the end of shift, please take my car to Granny's B 'n B. Park it out front where it can be easily seen."

"Will do boss."

He held the door open for me. "There you go, no more super cop for the day."

Secretly, I was happy to have him along."

CHAPTER TWENTY-FOUR

One of the perks of my job was the ability to order supplies, check staffing, discuss recipes, reconcile the cash drawer and come and go on my own schedule, within reason.

I dropped by Denise Young's house one morning to see how the newlyweds were adjusting. At least I told her that was why I was there. I took a dozen of Lewis's famous breakfast muffins.

The aromatic smell of cinnamon, cooked apples, and nutmeg made it almost impossible to fight the urge to open the box and have one on the way there.

"Hi, Denise, I brought you these." I handed her the pastries. "Have time for coffee? I got to thinking about how busy you were for months before the wedding. I thought maybe you could use coffee and conversation."

"Arizona, how sweet, please come in. I was about to have a cup of tea. These would be perfect, join me."

The most important thing was to make sure my visit didn't seem like an interrogation.

"I want to thank you again for listening to me at the book club meeting. I must have sounded like a lunatic thinking someone in my family could kill someone."

She had the condiments on the counter, rather than have her bring them to the table, I served myself. "Are the newlyweds settled somewhere?"

"Yes, they seem happy and have already begun the tradition of Sunday dinners with Mom and Dad. Now with Roger Freedman in the midst of moving here, I hope he joins us too."

I stirred my tea and took the paper off a muffin. "I didn't know he was moving here. What about his job and friends?" I never got over the irrational fear, when I lied, everyone could tell. "Between the brunch at your place and the wedding, we all flew to Boston for Ruth's funeral. Not many people attended. The papers were full of articles about her and how she *raped*, that's the word they used, raped, the fund her father and grandfather set up to feed the homeless."

She stopped and fooled around with the top of the breakfast treat. She took a small piece and nibbled on it. She looked like a mouse that wanted the cheese from a trap but wanted to keep its head. It gave me an opportunity to ask a question. "It's been nearly five weeks. What did Roger say? Do you think she did it?"

"Jackson and I ordered the Boston Globe online so we could follow the story. Seems churches, scout troops, and charities would write a grant to get money to feed the unfortunate. Ruth would approve the donation, write and sign the checks and keep half for herself. According to the paper, it had been going on for years. All I know about Roger is how embarrassed he was over the entire thing. He didn't have access to any of the money so he was cleared right away."

"How strange, did they find the money?"

"No Arizona, that's the strange part. The money vanished. The audit, according to the paper, began over a year ago. No one ever found a dime."

I finished my tea. "Do you think Roger is coming here to get away from the scandal?"

"Possibly, Dillon said all of his dad's clients left him over it. No one needs an accountant whose wife extorted millions of dollars. He has changed so much. He rarely says anything. It's as if his mind is always somewhere else, so sad."

"I wish he was a chef. We're looking for a third one at the restaurant. James and Lewis could use the help and it would give them the chance to get regular days off."

"Too bad I don't know anything about Roger Freedman's culinary skill, but Jackson is an amateur chef. Everywhere we went on vacation over the years, Jackson took a cooking lesson from a top school. He attended classes in Italy, France, Spain, Sweden, and all the big American schools.

"He has a passion for food. He kept track of all the classes he had taken. The best part of it is he loves to do the cooking."

"I'd better go. I have the lunch shift and it's

getting late. By the way, did Jackson end up with a diploma?"

She walked me to the door. "Yes, it was impressive. He walked across a stage with several other people at his level. He earned a certificate and a beautiful ring, silver if I remember correctly. As I said, it was a long time ago."

My heart pounded with excitement as I left the Young's.

On my way home I went by the Moonstone Reflection to see Liz Austin.

She had the phone to her ear and from her side of the conversation, I overheard, he *took anything not nailed down or locked up from the private boat slips on the north side of the lake.* She motioned for me to sit. The call didn't last long.

"How are you? It's been a couple of weeks. Every day I intend to come by for lunch."

"What keeps you away?"

"I'm writing a book about a battered woman who kills her abuser."

"Ouch, is that wishful thinking?"

"Not really. What brings you to the paper?" Liz paused to say hi to Nutmeg. "When I got the police log the other night it mentioned a robbery at the arcade. It was thwarted by a dog. Does that dog happen to be in the room with us?"

Nutmeg answered. "Arf."

"Yes, Keith Wesley and I were on our way to the Police Station to do some research when Nutmeg saw or heard something. She wanted out of the car at which time she apprehended the thief."

"She's one amazing dog. Do you mind if I do a

story on her?"

I reached down to pet my best friend. "I'm afraid a few things might happen. Someone might try to claim her, or she'll get hurt because people will be afraid of her, or people will try to test her abilities."

"Those are three good reasons. Is it okay to say a dog caught the robber if I don't even hint it was your dog?"

"If you promise. Have you had any news about the Freedman murder?"

"Funny you should ask. They convicted Ruth Freedman in absentia in the embezzlement of three-point- two million dollars, and some change. Authorities found the money in a bank account in Chicago under the name Zada Bacall."

I leaned forward in my chair. "How did they find the account?"

"A banker in Chicago recognized Ruth as Zada Bacall. He called the bank examiner who called the FBI. The story came over the wire about twenty minutes ago. It will be in tomorrow's paper." She looked around the room as if all the information was top secret. "The account had two beneficiaries." Liz looked through some papers on her desk. "Nero Yazi and Electra Amburgy."

"Do you have a piece of paper I can use? There's no way I'll remember those names."

She took a sheet of paper off of a tablet but instead of handing it to me she held it high in her hand. "On one condition and one condition only. You don't tell anyone what you learned here until it's verified. I don't know if your boyfriend the chief knows about this or not. Wait until it comes out in the paper tomorrow or you hear a news report about it. Chances are he already knows, but I like my job."

"I promise, and he's not my boyfriend. I'm not even sure I like him. By the way, how's your personal life?"

"Nonexistent. I may never date again and I know I won't try marriage again. I work, go to the gym, take long walks, read and now I'm writing, Violence In The Name of Love."

"Come by anytime and I'll buy your lunch."

As I left she whispered. "Not a soul, Arizona, not a soul."

CHAPTER Twenty-Five

We were busy at work. People came and went all day. Twice the waiting line snaked around the foyer and outside. I asked Aunt Sandy if we were having a special I didn't know about.

Most of the diners were the summer crowd. They wouldn't live at the lake full time until Memorial Day. This time of year someone from each family showed up to open the house, buy groceries, and be a general nuisance. And boy could they eat.

The biggest sellers every year, when they began to migrate, were hamburgers, cheeseburgers, French fries, and milkshakes. It did give James and Lewis a break. The line cooks made most of the simple foods.

I did a double take when Roger Freedman walked in. I decided to wait on him myself. "Welcome to our town. Good to have you here."

He gave me a half-smile, half-smirk and ordered.

After dinner, I took him coffee and he invited me

to sit down. "I'm sorry about earlier. I forget I'm not in Boston where when I went to my favorite places I got shunned. Next week I'll go back to doing my own cooking."

"Do you like to cook?"

He smiled for the first time. "I love to cook. I went to the American Culinary School in Anaheim when I first returned from the military and studied for six months in Italy. I even have a diploma."

Geez. Not another one. I was sure Jackson Young killed Roger's wife. I only needed to find out if he poisoned her and why, now someone else popped up. "Do you have one of those beautiful silver rings like my Chefs, James and Lewis?"

"Yes, I'm very proud of it. I did all the cooking when Dillon was growing up. I passed my love of the art to him also. He took a summer and traveled all over Europe to learn to cook. I was sure he would own his own restaurant one day.

"When he decided to go to law school he went to Chicago first to graduate from culinary school. He has a ring also. Come to think about it. I haven't seen him wear it lately. He probably took it off when he got married.

"One day I would like to see your kitchen and meet your chefs. The food here is excellent. Much better than one would expect considering the size of the town."

I took it as a backhanded compliment. The pause gave me a chance to slip out of the booth and get back to work.

Keith had been around every day, but when I had news, he was nowhere in sight.

What are the odds, Roger and Dillon Freedman and Jackson Young were all gourmet cooks?

This mystery got more complicated rather than less.

CHAPTER TWENTY-SIX

I jogged over to the north side to Pawsitivily Devine Dog Grooming for Nutmeg's bath and manicure. She loved the ritual but the ribbon they put in her hair, not so much.

While I waited I went into the Discount Grocery Store next door to get some junk food. It was a blessing to never have to cook or grocery shop but I loved junk food. There were no potato chips, and candy bars around the cafe. We didn't have Pop Tarts, Sugar Frosted Flakes, Oreos, Fig Newtons, or M&Ms.

Each time I took Nutmeg I went to the store and stocked up. The Discount Grocery Store wasn't big and the shelves were shorter than those in most other stores. I listened to the middle of a conversation between two women in the next aisle. One woman was a short brunette. Her hair hung straight down her back. She looked to be about forty, nicely groomed and well dressed.

The other lady was a bottle blond around the same age. She was dressed as though she had come from a yoga session to the store. Her body screamed fitness.

"I'm not happy he moved in next door to us. We've lived in that house for twenty-two years. Now we live next door to a killer," said the fit blond.

The brunette shot back an answer as though to defend the person they talked about. "You don't know if he's a killer or not."

The blond picked a head of cabbage, from the bin in front of her, and laid it on the produce scale. "Why else would he move to Moonstone Lake? He never comes out into the neighborhood. He invited Doug and me to a barbeque next Saturday night. I told Doug. I can't eat his food. What if he tries to poison us?"

The first lady quickly pushed her cart down the aisle. Over her shoulder she said. "He moved here to get away from the kind of bigotry you express right now. Albert and I will be there, and I know the Cramer's are going, I hope to see you."

I headed for the check out as the lady who said she would go to the BBQ rounded the corner. She nearly smashed into me.

I smiled and went on with my shopping.

Did everyone who knew who Roger Freedman was assume he killed his wife? Apparently, they didn't realize what a rascal she turned out to be. No one knew how she treated those of us who tried to help her with the wedding. And then there was the embezzlement.

Three men, Jackson Young, Dillon Freedman,

and Roger Freedman, all of them gourmet cooks; each of them knew how to disable Ruth to get her into the lake. I had an idea and needed to get to work as quickly as possible to see if I was right.

"Lewis, James, I need to ask you something."

They both came over to where I stood near the door. "It doesn't look busy, do you have time to take a break. I thought we could sit in the dining room."

Lewis asked. "Is everything okay?"

"Sure, I want to run an idea by you. Got time?"

Both men took off their aprons and torques and followed me to a table in the corner. "Can I have one of the guys bring you something?'

After we had iced tea all around, I asked my question. "Is there any food you can cook that would mimic cyanide? Something someone could eat and it could kill them, or if not kill them at least render them docile."

Lewis took a long drink of his tea. "My goodness, Arizona, there are so many I don't know where to start."

James said. "I'll start, raw almonds, cherries, potatoes, tomatoes, rhubarb, apples and mushrooms. Castor beans, bamboo shoots, and cassava root come to mind easily. If I wracked my brain, I could come up with some not so common ones."

"Come on, those are all common fruits, vegetables, and nuts. If it was that simple everyone would be dead. I eat those things all the time."

James shook his head. "Over the years, processes have been put into place for our safety. We don't eat raw almonds any more. They're warmed to get rid of the poison. Folks don't eat cherry pits or apple seeds in great quantities."

Lewis lifted his glass to get Matt's attention for a refill. "The three big ones he didn't mention, most likely on purpose."

"Okay guys, you have my attention. Which one would you use?"

Matt brought us salsa and chips. "Puffer fish is a big killer. The Japanese love it. Before a chef is allowed to serve it he has to study the fish for eight years. Then there are Castor beans, they can be smashed and sprinkled on things. That one's in the news a lot. Ricin, the white powder people are so afraid of. It'll kill you and is much easier to find or make. All you really need is a spice grinder. Last is Yam Beans, they are used in Thai food all the time. They'll kill you."

"Why would they use poisonous food in Thai cooking?" I asked.

James looked at Lewis. "I'll take this one. A Yam bean is a legume, unlike other legumes such as soybeans; these are grown for the tuberous root. You can use a young yam bean pod as a vegetable, but when they're mature they're poisonous. They act like cyanide. Remember though, chefs know food and can tell the difference between the different parts and ages of food. They know what not to put in the dish. People use the tuber and don't take a chance with the pods."

"Sure," James added. "If I were going to kill someone or make them extremely ill, I'd go for Yam Beans or Caster beans.

I slid out of the booth. "If either of you orders Yam Beans for the restaurant, I'm calling the police."

"Did I hear someone call for the police?" It was Keith.

I began to walk toward the front where Sandy had the drawer out to count it down. "As usual Chief, you are a day late and a dollar short."

"It's good to see you too, Ary."

Aunt Sandra looked up. "Are you two ever nice to one another?"

Me, "I'm always nice to him." And, him, "I'm always nice to her." came out at exactly the same time.

I turned my attention to Sandy. "Was the day as good as I think?"

She sat on the stool, kicked off her shoes, and wiggled her toes. "If my feet are any indication, it was marvelous."

Keith stood so close to me, I could feel his warm breath on my neck. "How did you get in here? We lock the doors before we take the drawer out."

Sandy looked up. "It's my fault. I let him in."

"You two are about to hurt my feelings. I came to talk about the Freedman murder."

I turned to look at him and at the same time, I pushed him back a step. Nutmeg had the same thought and almost tripped him as she came up beside me. "Are you hungry?"

He laughed. "I can always eat. Isn't the café closed?"

I headed toward the kitchen. "There are lots of leftovers around here and believe it or not, I'm a good cook." I walked around to the side of the counter with the refrigerators and cook tops. "Pick your poison."

He shook his hand as if he had been burned. "Ouch, I don't know if I want to eat here or not."

His jet black hair sparkled in the bright lights of the cooking arena. His salt and pepper sideburns added a distinguished heir to his appearance. When he turned playful and laughed his brown eyes disappeared into cute crinkled slits.

What I noticed gave me a warm glow from the tips of my toes to the top of my head.

Enough of that, I told myself.

"I make a mean grilled cheese and there's vegetable soup. How does that sound?"

"It sounds great." He leaned with one cheek on a stool on the other side of the counter. "Okay to sit here?"

"Sure, are you one of those people who can drink caffeine late and still sleep?"

"Yes, nothing bothers me. Where's the iced tea, I make a mean glass of sweet tea." He laughed at his own joke."

I pointed him in the right direction and went back to the grill. I decided I would let him tell me his news before I told him what I had learned. "Sorry, we'll have to eat in here. If we go into the dining room we'll get in the way of the cleaning crew. We are liable to get soapy mop water in our food. What's your news?"

He ate half his sandwich in two bites. "Sorry, I haven't eaten today. Ruth Freedman wasn't poisoned with cyanide. It was a common food. Either something not cooked that should have been or the part of a plant you aren't supposed to eat, a bushel of apple seeds and stuff like that."

"Keith, did it occur to you whoever did this might not have wanted to kill her, only disable her so they could get her into the water knowing she wouldn't have the strength to swim to shore?"

"No, it didn't. She was only a hundred yards offshore. Most anyone could dog paddle that far."

I got him a piece of apple pie, warmed it up and added some cinnamon ice cream. "Not fully dressed including shoes and a jacket, and disoriented by some foreign substance in your body messing with your head. I heard she might have had a heart attack before she went into the water."

He looked up. "Where did you hear that, Arizona? I got it straight from Dr. Stone and I haven't told anyone. Did you go visit the Medical Examiner ?"

I chose not to answer and went on to something else. "I dropped by to see Denise Young under the guise of checking on the newlyweds. During the conversation, I found out Jackson Young is a gourmet cook and has a ring like the one Nutmeg found at the shoreline.

"Earlier Roger Freedman came in for dinner. I chatted with him a little while and found out he and Dillon both have one of those rings and are amateur chefs. Anyone of the three of them could have rendered her helpless and threw her in the lake."

"This pie is delicious. Even though she's dead, the State of New York declared her guilty of embezzling a couple of million dollars."

"I know, and they found the money too."

He walked to the sink and rinsed the dishes. "How do you know that? I read it off the line before I came over here. No one else could have that information.

It was one of the things I wanted to tell you.

"I haven't seen you in a while. I thought we could take a ride over to the station and see if we could track down the strange names of the people who were the beneficiaries of the money."

I reached into my pocket and took out my note. "You mean, Nero Yazdi and Electra Amburgy?"

Keith walked over until he stood directly in front of me. He rested his hands on his hips. "Arizona, first the heart attack, then the money and now you have the names of the beneficiaries. Where did you get those names? This is hush-hush. If those names get out, they might go underground, we may never find them."

Aunt Sandy walked by, saw us and came into the kitchen. "What do you two have your heads together about?"

I looked at Keith, he shook his head yes. "We came across two strange names. They may have something to do with Ruth Freedman's murder. We don't know who they are?"

She sat on the stool next to Keith. He nodded to me again and I read to her from the paper. "Nero Yazdi and Electra Amburgy, do they mean anything to you?"

She went to the fridge, opened the door to look in. "Is there any more pie? If I have to think, I need food."

"I can tell the names are familiar to you." I fixed Sandra a piece of pie and a second one for Keith. I took time to warm each slice and add ice cream. "There's your pie, now tell us you don't know who they are."

She smiled and took a bite. "Electra Amburgy was a young girl from a novel. I don't remember much about the book but the name has always stayed with me. It came out in the seventies. She was mean and spiteful. It took place at a summer camp where she played tricks on the other campers. Karma got her in the end. With a name like hers, I believe you won't have any problem finding out more about her.

"Nero Yazdi is another child from a book. Again it was the name, Nero the Hero. I remember it to have been dystopian. He was the child of a couple who was out to destroy an evil monarch. Inadvertently the child took over for them and became the hero. Neither book stood out as great literature. I belong to nine book clubs. Someone chose it. I couldn't say much because sometimes no one cares for the books I pick, but they read them anyway.

"I'm not trying to get in your business, but if someone has used those names in some legal, or illegal matter, they are being funny. Those are two names you won't find in the real world.

"I hope I helped. My feet tell me it's time to head home and let Wynken, Blyken, and Nod, lay on them."

Keith looked my way as if for an explanation. "Her cats," I said.

I whistled for Nutmeg who had been asleep under the podium. "Since there isn't really anything to research now, I believe I'll take my dog for a walk and call it a day. Seems like Sunday Brunch comes more often than once a week."

He looked at his watch. "It's late and I see no reason to drive back across town. Mind if I join you and Nutmeg."

Nutmeg wagged her tail. Boy, I thought. She has made an about face.

The first part of our walk was quiet. I loved my walks around the lake. Since I walked alone most of the time, the silence seemed natural to me.

Keith asked, "How many people do you think have chef's rings or whatever they're called? It seems a might odd all three of the men we're looking at for Ruth's murder have them."

"Add at least two more. Both of my chefs have them. There has to be more evidence out there and we're missing it."

"So, Miss Private Eye, what's your idea?"

"To find out who likes Thai food and who likes to cook it."

"Why Thai food?"

"I'm convinced our victim ate yam beans. It's a hunch I have and most usually I'm right when I have as strong a feeling as I do now."

He stopped and looked at me. "Are you always like this?"

"Like what?"

"All work and no play."

I could feel my defenses go up. "I work and run and love to solve mysteries."

"Do you like to go out to dinner?"

"Not usually. I consider it a busman's holiday. In this case, I would love to go if we can make it a Thai Restaurant."

"Is there one in Moonstone Lake?"

"Yes, it's in the downtown district on the north side of the lake. It'll be an adventure. I don't go many places I have to go in a vehicle."

"Tuesday evening okay?"

"Tuesday evening is wonderful. By the way, I dropped by the grocery store today and overheard a conversation about Roger Freedman inviting people to a cookout on Saturday. I say we crash it and see what he's like in his own element."

"Geez, Ary, that wouldn't be nice. Besides, how would you go about it?"

"Since it's a week away, we have plenty of time to plan. I'll have the guys make some special dish and we'll drop by and give it to him as a housewarming gift."

"Wonderful idea, I'm sure he won't think anything is out of the ordinary when you show up with the police in a cruiser."

I stopped and turned to face him. "First of all, you don't have to wear a uniform. It's a Saturday night. Chief Chase only wore his to court, funerals, and parades. Secondly, it's only a mile or a mile and a half over there." I patted his belly lightly. "Looks like you could use a little exercise."

He looked down at his stomach and said. "That wasn't nice."

I Googled the two weird names on the bank account. I concluded she had no thought of anyone picking up the money but her. If I looked hard enough, I could most likely track her and discover her get-a-way plan.

CHAPTER TWENTY-SEVEN

The Moonstone Lake Café had been having a Sunday Brunch each week for over sixty years. The cooks, servers, food, and chefs had changed over the years but by and large, we had the same routine week after week.

This Sunday was different. First, at one booth, someone loosened the lids on the salt and pepper shakers and a lady smothered her food with black pepper.

Things ground to a halt while I grabbed Sandy and we visited every table to make sure it wouldn't happen somewhere else.

Later someone put mustard in the catsup bottles, on top of the catsup. Again, we grinded to a stop while we made sure no one else would ruin his French fries.

I took a break to see how things were going with Aunt Sandy, and I could see kids climbing into the fountain outside the front door, stealing quarters as fast as they could.

Nutmeg went out to handle that one. She walked around the boys at the fountain and growled at each one. She pulled one kid out of the water by his belt. It didn't take them long to leave.

Tourist season had started. It took the part-timers a couple of days to settle into small village mentality.

When I was sure it couldn't get any more chaotic, Mother sashayed in dressed as if she were about to sing at a Mexican wedding. She wore a fiesta dress, platform wedges to match and castanets on each thumb.

I cut her off at the door, "Mom. What are you doing?"

"Sorry I'm late, I decided to take you up on your offer to be a traveling hostess and chat with the guests."

I tried my best not to sound alarmed. "Why are you dressed in those clothes?"

"Marsha and I are exploring the different places we might go on our trip. Mexico is close, we may go there. If not, we'll explore another country."

Aunt Sandy cleared her throat. When I looked her way, she shook her head no. "Emma, you look delightful, I'm sure the guests will be thrilled to see you."

I stood flabbergasted. "Sure, Mom, they'll be thrilled." After she left for the dining room I asked Sandy, "what if she plays those things on her thumbs?"

"Lighten up, Arizona. She'll be fine so long as she doesn't fall off her platform shoes."

I went to the kitchen and looked out the doorway to see how she was received. Truthfully, it was the most laughter and frivolity I'd heard in the dining room for a long while.

I only hoped Mom and Martha didn't decide to try Hawaii and Mother showed up in a grass skirt and coconuts for a top.

CHAPTER TWENTY-EIGHT

The Thai Garden Restaurant had been in Moonstone Lake for years. I had never been there. Keith had gone to the trouble to make a reservation.

Once we were seated, the waiter brought two small colorful teapots of Jasmine tea. I poured a cup, leaned over and took a deep breath, it smelled of lily-of-the-valley and sweet woodruff.

I was excited to see the menu so I could see if yam beans were listed. They were not.

"What are you going to have?" Keith asked. "I don't see your poison plant as a choice. I can't say I'm not relieved."

"I guess I'll ask him about it."

The waiter let us sip our tea and explore the entrees before he came back to the table. "What can I get for you tonight?"

I went first. "Do you have anything with yam beans?"

"No ma'am."

Keith looked up. "You don't have yam beans?"

"I'm not familiar with the term yam bean. If it is important, I will ask our chef, Aroon."

Keith looked at me. "That would be great. We have heard about them and had our hearts set on tasting them."

A few minutes later a man came out the kitchen door and walked to our table. I guessed he was the chef. He didn't dress as formally as mine. "He spoke with a thick accent but remained easy to understand. "You and the young lady would like to taste something with yam bean?"

I answered, "yes, we would."

"I don't know where you learned about this plant, but we don't use it here. The bigger cities where they have access to it daily so it is young and fresh still use it, but we do not."

Keith asked him, "is it dangerous?"

"Yes sir, it is. Mostly it is used as a legume only by people who grow it or can get it fresh. It is a concern if an older pod is opened and the beans cooked. Most of us use the root. It became popular because water chestnuts are scarce. Sliced, it tastes nearly the same. It is called jicama."

We looked at each other and I shrugged my shoulders. "I always thought it was a Mexican product."

"Actually, miss, the plant originated from Africa and made a big circle around the globe. It has become popular in the United States. I hope this helps you and you are not too disappointed to stay and dine with us."

I picked up the menu. "I'm not familiar with the food so I am not sure what to order."

"Enjoy your tea. I will make you a meal you will never forget." He bowed and left.

The waiter kept smiling.

I poured another cup of tea. "What disturbs me is that my chefs didn't tell me or make the distinction between the two parts of the plant. Do you think they did it on purpose?"

He put his hand on top of mine. I took it as a gesture of understanding so I left my hand where it was. "I don't think they did. I don't think I've seen any jicama around your place and you said more than once, the bean. They made an honest determination."

"You're probably right."

Our dinner was superb, Thai chicken salad, Tom Yam Kei-a sweet and sour soup with chili and lime. The main course consisted of Salmon with spices, wrapped in a tortilla, covered with cheese and lime juice. Devine is all I could say about the entire meal.

Keith finished before I did. "Do they have coffee here?"

"I'm sure they do, but since we're going all out, there's a Starbucks two blocks down and hot chi latte is my favorite."

He called the waiter and told him we were finished. I offered to pay half of the bill but he wouldn't hear of it.

It became a moot point because the chef wouldn't take any money. I left four buffet passes for the waiter, the chef, whoever they wanted to bring. I wondered if they considered eating out on their day off as a busman's holiday also.

Nutmeg waited patiently in the car. Keith put the back window down a few inches but it wasn't safe to leave the car unlocked with the shotgun, long gun, and radio in the front seat.

I had no doubt if Nutmeg wanted out of the car, she would unlock the doors. And Keith's equipment was safe even with the doors wide open. Nutmeg would have seen to it.

I let her out and she ran around us several times and off to the bushes. When she finished her business, she jumped back into the car ready to go.

The next morning I asked James about the jicama. "Truthfully, Arizona, I have been here doing this for a couple of years, before that I owned a catering business. Jicama wasn't something I thought about when we were discussing poison foods. All I know about yam beans is what I learned in cooking school fifteen years ago. I can, however, tell you what the latest trends in café and buffet menu set up are."

When James came to Moonstone Lake Café two years ago, he never mentioned he once had a catering company. He didn't exactly say it, but I got the idea he came to us straight out of the Army.

Lewis sauntered in from the storage room. "I heard most of your conversation and I'm inclined to agree. Once in a while I see something that looks interesting and I try it, but I'm to the point in my life I like to go home, visit with my kids, play with my new grandbaby, and work in the garden. I do enjoy my work here and as James does, I keep abreast of the new items making the rounds. Sorry we weren't more help last night."

"I understand. While you are both here, it's time

to change the menu and desserts for the summer crowd. They're already fussing about fried okra and ham and beans. How soon will you two be ready to talk about any new dishes and what we should add for summer?"

James looked at Lewis. "We'll be ready in the morning, what about you?"

It was settled. We would go over the menu and I would order supplies, with their help. The summer buffet would be ready, even though it wasn't yet spring.

Lewis added, "Ary, come tomorrow morning with an open mind. We want to change some of the buffet this year."

I didn't answer. I waved as I left.

My mind reverted to Ruth Freedman and the money. I made up my mind the money was the key to the killer. I had heard the statement *follow the money*, thousands of times. It didn't get popular by accident.

I lay in bed, petted Nutmeg and made a mental list of murder motives on the ceiling with my mind.

Greed was first; love gone wrong came in second. I tried to picture Ruth Freedman in a love triangle, I couldn't. Then it hit me, revenge. She had stolen millions of dollars. People were hurt, entire organizations had no money to buy food for the disadvantaged. It lengthened the list of those who might want her dead.

If she could take the money without any concern for what it did to those who depended on it, I wondered who else she might have destroyed.

I'd never seen Mrs. Freedman be nice or polite to

anyone, not even her son. I kept going back to the money. It had to take all of her mental capabilities and concentration to redirect so much money from one bank to another.

One bank to another, it dawned on me, I didn't know which bank she sent the money to.

A bank in Chicago under the name Zada Bacall was all I knew. There had to be hundreds of banks in Chicago. I wished I had asked Sandra if she knew the name, Zada Becall, when she identified the other two. I wanted to ask her but I glanced at the clock and it flashed 2:30 am. I made a mental note to ask her in the morning and went to sleep.

I had a restless night. A young female camper came to the café and played mean tricks on the customers. We were saved by a young boy named Hero who ran her off. When I got up to go on my morning run, I didn't feel as if I had been asleep all night. Maybe I hadn't.

I'd been a runner since high school. Kids picked on me about my bony legs, skinny arms, bright red hair, and size eleven feet. When I ran, all of the jeering and teasing faded away. Cross country was my event.

A feeling came over me when I ran. My dreams were reality as I led the pack at every meet. I could create a mom and dad who loved me, I ran for student council and won, Johnny Mason (the cutest boy in the school) asked me to prom, and I, like the other girls, talked about food and how to lose a little weight when that time of the month came.

Every day when I finished my runs on the team, the only accolades I received were from the track coach as the stars of the other girls cross country teams fell to the wayside as I broke their records one by one.

My thoughts were disrupted when Nutmeg began to bark. I followed her line of sight and spied Keith jogging toward us. I stopped, "It everything okay?"

He leaned down and petted Nutmeg, who wagged her tail. Her attitude toward him had certainly changed. "I decided you were right about my waist line. When I thought it over, running in the morning would fit best in my schedule. Do you mind?"

"No, will you keep it up when you get to your new house?"

"Sure, I guess I never told you where it is. It's one of those small homes across from the Lake Side Cabins on Sunshine Street."

I didn't mean to laugh, I couldn't help myself. "You bought a house on the lake, two blocks down the street from Roger Freedman?"

"At the time I bought it, I had no idea he'd move to Moonstone Lake. After all of the trouble I've had getting the house up to the standard it was supposed to be when I signed the contract. I am not selling."

"What does the house look like? I have been jogging the path long enough to have them all memorized."

"It's the white one with red shutters and a blue door. It reminds me a little of a sailboat."

"Oh, Keith, I love that house. You did good, and as a plus, you can have a beer with Roger."

"I hope you get over that joke soon." He began to jog and looked back at me. "Are you going to run or stand there and stare at me?"

"Come on Nutmeg. Let's see if he can keep up."

CHAPTER TWENTY-NINE

Two hours later I sat in the kitchen with James and Lewis. Their excitement for whatever they were working on electrified the room. I glanced down at the table where catalogs, recipes, a pan of hot cinnamon rolls, and a rolled up sign or drawing took up all the space.

Lewis put the largest roll on a plate and slid it over in front of me. "Is that mine? What a tasty surprise? What's all this stuff? I've never seen you two go to this much trouble to make a menu change."

James served himself a pastry. "In reality, we're sucking up to you. We know your favorite flavor is cinnamon. Why else would you ask for cinnamon sprinkled on top of your apple pie when there is a gob inside and order cinnamon ice cream when most people don't know it exists. Notice Lewis gave you the one with the most icing."

"Why suck up? Now I'm worried you might want to change us to a Chinese drive through. Let's see your ideas. You've done a bang up job for us so far."

"Okay," James answered, "I guess we have buttered you up enough."

"Come on gentlemen, I'm easy to work with. You have both told me so. We'd better get started."

James unrolled a large drawing of the dining room featuring a buffet. It was nothing like the setup we had. "We would like to modernize the dining room with a new buffet. Now before you have a fit about cost, let us tell you what and why."

I stood to look at the detailed plans but all I saw were dollar signs. Since I didn't want to shut them down, I took a bite of my pastry, stirred my coffee and sat back to listen.

Lewis took over. "We have been studying all of the latest trends in our industry. Instead of separate dishes, the modern buffets are going with specialized bars."

James put his finger on one end of the drawing. "This is where our salad bar is now. We wouldn't change it much. The change there would be a new station to match the rest of the new equipment. This section is a taco bar. It would have seasoned ground beef, taco shells, shredded cheese, tomatoes, onions, shredded lettuce, queso sauce, salsa and chips. We've been talking about shredded chicken too. I forgot to do a cost analysis on adding chicken. I'll have it by this afternoon."

Lewis took over. "Tex-Mex is the second most popular fast food after hamburgers and fries."

James put a finger on the next section. "This area

would be the pasta bar, three kinds of noodles, six different sauces, cheese, and meat balls."

It was like a tennis match, James, Lewis, James, Lewis.

Lewis took his turn. "This would house the all-important pizza bar. One good thing about a pizza bar is dessert pies. I can make cherry, strawberry, and almost any other pizza you can think of, including cinnamon."

James added. "We need some favorites and old standbys, Waldorf salad, fresh fruit, old fashioned green beans with bacon, fried chicken, catfish, mashed potatoes, cream pies, Jell-O, small cakes and cookies, and a new featured dessert each week."

Lewis let out a deep breath he must have taken so he could carry on. "Over here is the sundae bar, a soft serve machine with chocolate, vanilla, and swirl. This tray will hold the toppings, our research shows these to be the most popular- chocolate, hot fudge, caramel, strawberry and butterscotch. The special add-ons would be brownie bits, Oreo bits, peanut butter cup bits, sprinkles, chocolate chips and gummy bears."

"What do you think?" They said almost simultaneously.

"I love it. Let's go mark it off in comparison to the old one. It looks smaller. One thing I don't want is to crowd people so they are shoulder to shoulder."

We spent the next hour with a tape measure and tape to see how the new system would fit.

"I do have one question," I said. "If hamburgers are so popular, why aren't there burgers, buns and French fries and condiments somewhere?"

James answered, "All we would have to do is make the fish warmer narrower and buy one more tray for the meat. Condiments can be at the end of the bar."

The dining room got busy while we measured and kibitzed. We finished our conversation in the kitchen. I waved my hand over the entire picture they had presented. "Then I guess we need to get down to the nitty-gritty. How much is the new buffet equipment? How long would it take us to switch over? How long before we get a figure on the cost of the food or do you have all of the ingredients worked out?"

We spent four hours working on the new concept. All the concerns were addressed. Finally, they both stopped talking and looked at me.

"I love it and we'll do it. As a courtesy I'll run it by Mom and Sandy. I can do that this evening. The sooner we figure out the logistics the better. I think if we are going to redo the entire thing, we should paint. The floors have been in here since I was a kid. I want to put a new one down.

"Maybe we could find a buyer for the old system. Write up the order for the bar, I'll figure the paint and flooring. I would want to close down after a Sunday brunch at two and reopen with everything finished on a Tuesday morning.

"This will take a goodly amount of planning and co-ordination. If all of your cost analysis is correct, we should make the money back pretty quickly."

Change wasn't something I embraced, but I knew these innovations would take us into the new century.

I nearly made it to the door toward my apartment

when Liz came in. "Hey girl, I came in to take you up on that lunch."

I glanced at my watch. "That's great. The place is running like a well-oiled machine today so I was going to take the afternoon off."

She deflated in front of me. "Don't let me hold you up. I should have called first."

I walked toward her. "No, I meant I have all of the time in the world to visit with you." I gave her a hug. "Glad you're here."

We took a booth toward the back. I sat on the far side facing out. "Do you still have a fetish about someone sitting behind you?"

"Yes and I still have no reason for it. How's it going at the paper? Any scandals I should know about?"

"Did you know Ruth Freedman had a complete other identification?"

"You mean Zada Bacall?"

"Yes, but not only the name, a social security card, and an apartment in Chicago."

I tried not to let my mouth hang open. "No kidding! Does Keith know?"

"I'm sure he does. It came over the wire yesterday evening."

We were interrupted by Matt who came to take our order. "What's the lunch special?" She asked. "Oh, never mind. I'd really like a cup of tomato basil soup, a grilled cheese on rye, and a diet Pepsi."

He looked toward me. "I think I'll feed my sweet tooth. Bring me a piece of the triple chocolate cake I saw back there, bring two. My friend would like one also."

There was no way Liz could complain. What little weight she had on her before, she lost when she lived with Mick Dudley.

"Want to go to the boat dock with me? It's been three months since the murder and my editor wants to keep the story in the news cycle so it doesn't become a cold case."

"Sure, I'll go. What are you taking pictures of?"

"I thought the wooden landing down to the boat slip, the slip itself, and then the calm water where you spotted the body. It's not much but then we don't have much. I'm going to put a picture of Ruth in the article also."

"With all my heart, I thought hubby did it, but now I'll have to rethink it because of her second life in Chicago. Maybe she hated her life and wanted to get away from it, so she took the money, got a new identity and intended to live happily ever after as Zada Bacall.

"Or a person we haven't identified and isn't on our list, found out about her plan. He tried to blackmail her. When she didn't pay up, he lost his temper and killed her."

Liz stopped eating her soup. "It could have gone down like that, but why would you kill her if you couldn't get access to the money? There has to be another reason."

"Ary, I have a question. When we first talked about this, you found her wedding ring and a glove. Why has there never been any mention of the glove?"

I put both hands on the table. "Some detective I am. After we eat, we can go and ask the chefs if they remember it. There's also the chance Keith took it. I wouldn't put it past him."

I sat and toyed with my dessert. Liz ate without uttering another word. I could not remember what I did with the glove. I picked the ring up, saw the glove and took it too. Why did I draw a blank after that? Mother took the ring, maybe she took the glove. No she took the gold ring, this was the silver one.

Matt dropped by to re-fill our glasses and bring Liz's cake.

She looked at it and her eyes got big. "Oh my goodness, is this death by chocolate, or what?"

"It's Lewis' new chocolate cake recipe with some extras, he only makes it once in a while for our restaurant family. It's not cost effective to serve to patrons. Mom thought we should make it and use it to recognize diners on their birthdays. We could give them a piece of this cake with a candle in it. Unless you have a gigantic sweet tooth or have a huge family, one piece is enough for everyone to have a bite."

She stuck her fork in it and took a taste. "I would love to have this recipe, but from the taste, I'd say it's complicated."

"The first layer is chocolate cake, the second is chocolate mousse, the third is fudge, and the fourth is mousse again then another thin layer of cake. It has cream cheese icing which he also chose to make fudgy. Let's go to the kitchen, get you a to-go box and ask around about the glove."

No one claimed having seen it.

Nutmeg raced through the door on a dead run. She slid as she tried to stop in front of James and knocked him off his feet in her exuberance. She wasn't allowed in the kitchen and I'd never seen her aggressive for no reason. She began to paw at a door under the cabinets at his station.

James stood, wiped the flour off his pants, walked to the cabinet and pushed my dog out of the way. The entire scene ran in slow motion. Nutmeg wanted in the door and had no intention of moving.

James tried to stay between her and the door. "Whatever she smells must be pretty appealing to dogs. Maybe she's hungry."

Lewis joined us. "I doubt there's food under there. I pray it isn't a mouse."

James leaned on the counter in front of the door. "I'll take care of it." He looked over to me. "If anyone sees Nutmeg in this kitchen, we'll have to close down and clean. It's a huge no-no, with the potential of causing us unneeded work."

My mind went blank. What I wanted to do was order him to open the door and let us see its contents. I ruled out dog food the instant he said it. A thousand thoughts ran through my mind. He could be a closet drinker and kept liquor in the cabinet. It could, indeed, be a mouse.

If I learned one thing in my time on earth, it was step back, don't push. James had been in the kitchen for nearly two years His work ethic and cooking skills were impeccable. I decided to give him the benefit of the doubt.

My mind agreed with me but my body betrayed me. I had to hold one hand in the other to keep them from trembling. I couldn't stop the flush that started in my toes and sky rocketed to my brain.

I took hold of Nutmeg's collar. She had no

intention of moving away from the door on her own. "Sorry James, I know she shouldn't be in here." She pulled against me for the first time. "Nutmeg. Now."

The dog whined, backed away a few steps and sat. She barked loudly four or five times. Lewis put his hand on my shoulder. "Arizona, he's right. The dining room is full. Someone is bound to come in here to investigate if she keeps it up."

I sat the remainder of my cake on the counter, as did Liz. We took the dog out the back door to avoid the customers.

The door closed behind me and I leaned on it. "What do you make of that?"

Liz stepped between me and a small table we had set up for the employee's breaks. "I think James has a secret, and it's in the cabinet he guarded so valiantly. You handled the situation professionally. I'm proud of you."

I rubbed Nutmeg's ears with my still shaking hands. "I'm sorry girl. Sometimes we have to bow to the rules. I'll let you search later once we're closed for the night."

Liz knelt down by the dog. "Maybe he drinks and has a bottle under there?"

"It's the first thought that went through my mind too."

My dog stunned me again when she made a low grunt and shook her head *no*."

"Arizona, I don't know if your dog is amazing or scary. Can I ask her a question?"

"Sure, why not?"

"Nutmeg, do you like James?"

A head shake *no*.

"Who's your best friend?"

She walked over and put a paw on me

"I think your dog is a human reincarnated sent to you for some reason we don't yet understand."

"Do you believe in reincarnation?" I asked.

"I wasn't sure until I met Nutmeg."

The three of us walked around to the front of the building. When I opened the front door Nutmeg ran to the podium and lay under it.

I told Liz, "I'm not sure I can go to the dock with you right now. I want to hang out in the kitchen and make sure James doesn't take anything out of those lower cabinets. I'll go with you tomorrow."

"How do you know he didn't take it out already while we were outside?"

"I saw the look on Lewis' face. I'm not the only one who thought James' behavior strange. He would tell me." I gave her a big hug.

She smiled. "I can take care of the pictures. Just make sure you let me know what happens. I want to know what's in that cabinet."

Every nerve in my body fired at once. What on earth had happened in the kitchen? My heart said it couldn't be much because of how well I knew James. I stayed in the restaurant and close to the galley until Lewis and James, and the crew, were gone for the night.

In my heart I knew nothing would ever be the same at Moonstone Lake Café and Sunday Brunch and it made me sad.

I walked around as I did every night when I closed. I made sure no burners or ovens were on, no electrical appliances were plugged in, the walk-in freezer lights were off and no diner remained to play havoc with the place after we left.

The magazine, Restaurant Today, once told the story of a homeless man who lived in a café for two months before anyone found him. He hid in the pantry behind all the boxes until everyone left. He was careful only to take small portions of the food left in the refrigerator and drink tap water, never coffee or tea.

I never begrudged anyone who needed food, I did oppose people who hid in the business where they could get hurt or scare the bee-gee-bees out of the people who worked there.

On Lewis' way home each night, he took any and all food we were not going to use the next day and dropped it off at the homeless camp.

CHAPTER THIRTY

Sandy locked the front door before she ran her tape and counted the drawer. I stood by the back door and let each person out with a friendly *good night, thanks for your hard work. See you tomorrow*.

James had asked a dozen times in the last two years if he could have the code to the pass through door so he could go to his apartment without going outside.

I said no. If for some reason the outside door to our apartment building didn't get locked or someone broke in, I wanted the security system on.

We set the first part of the alarm when the front door was locked, the second part when the last employee exited and the main section when we walked out the common door to our apartments.

It was bad enough Mother knew how to come and go. It led to events like the cookie eating binge and the time she let her friends in the backdoor and they played cards on the kitchen prep counters and ate all of the cookies and desserts for the next day. I had to call Lewis in on his day off to help out.

James was the last to leave. He mumbled a good night and I locked the door behind him.

I looked up when I heard Nutmeg walk across the floor. She sat at my feet and leaned on me.

Since I knew nothing about dogs when mine adopted me, I read a book about them. When they lean they are anxious, want you to go somewhere, or show they love you. Why couldn't it be one thing so I knew what she wanted?

Sandy came in from the front with the cash and receipts in the bank bag. "I've balanced within ten cents for the last week. When Patty worked the other night she came within fifty cents. I'd say that's pretty good.

"Why do you look like you just lost your best friend? I haven't seen Keith around today, you two on the outs?"

"He is *not* my boyfriend. We happen to share a common interest in crime and he doesn't know many people in town."

"Why the sad face?"

"It's James. Today Nutmeg had a fit trying to get something out of James' work station. He stood in front of it and offered no explanation for what the dog might be going after. It kind of blew over, but I have had the urge to throw up ever since. I think something's wrong."

"Did you look to see what it was?"

"No, I'm kind of afraid. Nutmeg went crazy and James acted guilty. Do you think he's a closet drinker?"

"Let me put the money in the safe, and we'll look."

"I'm torn. If he has some personal secret, maybe we shouldn't pry."

"Arizona. Look at your hands shake. Are you going to be able to work with James if you don't know what it is?"

Nutmeg ran to the cabinet she went to earlier in the day. She sniffed and whined then pawed the same door as before. I sat on the floor and opened both doors. The dog stepped over me and dug to the back. She pulled out pots and pans as she went. "Move Nutmeg, I'll get it. You're making a mess. Every one of those utensils you touched will have to be washed."

She made a noise I hadn't heard before and moved away.

Sandy sat on a stool and watched. "Find anything?"

"Not yet."

"It's a bag, it's soft." I pulled it out. A brown paper bag rolled up with a rubber band around it. When I unrolled it and pulled the item out, I had to catch my breath.

Sandy stood. "What is it?"

"It's a glove."

"That's it, a glove."

"Not just any glove, Sandy. It's the leather glove I found with the ring near the lake. Why would he hide it? I hope it isn't the obvious reason."

"And what's that?"

"If the ring and glove belong to James, for some

unknown reason, he might have killed Ruth Freedman."

"Come on, Arizona. This is James, the James who fixed you chicken soup when you were sick, and the same James who took care of you when hot grease fell on your hand. I'm sure there's a good explanation. Ask him what it is."

I took the bag and glove and set it on the table near her. No matter how long I stared at it I couldn't get my head around what it might mean. "Here's my dilemma. If the ring and glove belong to James, he's most likely a murderer. Whoever killed Ruth Freedman knew enough about food to incapacitate her so she couldn't fight while he put her in the lake."

"Why would he want to kill her?"

"I don't know if he did it. If I take the glove he'll know I figured it out. If I leave the glove and he destroys it, I'll have no evidence. I'm between a rock and a hard place."

"Call Keith, he's a cop, he'll know what to do. Have him come over and tell him all of this. I believe there's a good explanation for what you said happened today. Until you guys figure it out, I would cover my butt just in case James turns out to be someone we don't know, and he did the dirty deed. I need to go see about the cats. Are you okay?"

Aunt Sandy hugged me and petted Nutmeg. I went to the common door with her, let her out and locked it behind her.

Never before had I been uncomfortable or spooked in the diner alone. All my life it had been my home. I sat in a booth in the corner with my back to the wall in case my jitters were justified.

Nutmeg sat beside me with her head on my lap. Allowed or not allowed, I intended to keep the dog with me.

I checked the time, nine-fifteen, still early enough to call Keith. "Hi, are you at Granny's?"

He was not. I interrupted the first night in his new home.

"I need to talk to you about something. I'm in the restaurant. It's important. Call me when you get to the front door and I'll let you in."

It seemed less than a minute before my phone rang and it was him. I kept him on the phone all the way to the door. I checked out the window before I opened it. When he stepped in, I stuck my head out and looked both ways before I locked it again.

He looked at me, took a step closer and hugged me. "My goodness Arizona, what happened?"

I took his hand and guided him to the booth where I had been sitting. I slipped in my side and he took the seat across from me. "Okay, you're pale, your hands are freeing and you're shaking. What happened? Did someone try to rob you?"

"No, it's about James."

I told him the entire story from the first time Nutmeg ran into the kitchen to when Sandra and I found the glove in a paper bag.

He put his hand on mine. "I don't blame you for being scared and not knowing what to do. We'll work this out. We need to put the glove back in the bag and the bag back where you found it. First, I'll photograph it. Will you let me out so I can grab a fingerprint kit. I left it in the car. I don't want to call a CSI crew since he lives here. We don't want to play our hand until we are sure we have a good one. He might have an explanation, but if he did, why didn't he open the door?

"Once we've documented our find, we'll put it back and act as though nothing happened. When he figures out its still where he left it, he'll relax. Meanwhile, we'll try to connect him to Ruth.

"We also have to bear in mind the glove doesn't mean he killed her. The only real clue is that for some reason he hid the glove. It's quite a mystery on its own."

Keith took dozens of pictures. "Okay, Ary, let's put this all back together. Can you fix it so he won't know we found the glove?"

"I think so."

By the time we were done I was drained. The stress of watching James all evening, and the worry he might have done something horrible took its toll on me.

Keith and I sat on the bench in front of my apartment building while Nutmeg took herself for a walk.

The Chief walked me to the front door. Right then my knees buckled. "I totally forgot he lives right below me. He could be waiting for me."

"I doubt Nutmeg will let him near you but I'll be right here. When you get upstairs and are safely locked in, call me. I'm not offering to go with you because I don't want him to jump to the conclusion you called me about the glove."

"But he doesn't know that."

"He would if I walked you to your door."

"You're probably right."

Keith gave me another hug. He looked toward the front door and said in a low even voice. "James is standing at the front window watching us. Don't panic. I'm going to kiss you goodnight so he thinks this is a date."

He leaned down, found my lips and kissed me. A gentle, caring, kiss a woman wants on a first date. It felt so right and warm I nearly forgot why he kissed me. I reach up, put my arms around his neck, and played with the hair at his neckline. He kissed me again and I came back to the moment. "I'm so sorry, Keith. I didn't…"

He put a finger lightly on my lips, "I'm not. Come on I'll walk you to the door. I don't see him now. I don't think he would take a chance to run into Nutmeg in the hallway. Who lives where in the building?"

"As you face it, Mom's on the bottom left, James is bottom right, I'm top left and Sandy is top right."

"Do you have to walk up or is there an elevator?"

My legs trembled and my head spun, I didn't know if it was the kiss or James. It didn't seem to bother him. "Stairs."

"Okay, same plan. I'll walk you to the door, and you call me as soon as you're upstairs and safe." He smiled and touched my cheek. "It doesn't matter if he's Jack the Ripper, or just a weird guy who took the glove for some silly reason we don't know. I won't let anything happen to you." He gave me a peck on the cheek, took my hand, and led me to the door. I pressed the proper numbers to get in and said good night.

"Arizona, how much do you trust me?"

"That's a strange question. If I didn't trust you, I would not have called you."

"I need the code to this door in case of an emergency. I might need to get in. Do you use the same codes for all the doors even the ones in the restaurant?"

"Only Mom, Sandra, and I have the security codes to the pass through door and the back and front door of the restaurant are the same. This door is different and only we four tenants know the code for this door."

"So James doesn't need a key, a code gets him in?"

"Yes and all the doors inside have a deadbolt. I have a key to all of the apartments. At times like this I wonder if my mom should have access the restaurant security.

"James can come in the front door here but he doesn't have the code to use the pass through door. It has been a point of contention with him since he started. I've let him through a couple of times in bad weather. He always stood close to me. I bet he wanted to see the numbers. It made me uncomfortable."

"You didn't answer my question. I may need to get in this door."

I didn't hesitate to give it to him. Was I naïve? "815135"

He took a note pad out of the back pocket of his jeans and wrote it down. "815135, it isn't an anniversary or birthday, something easy to guess is it?"

"No. I made the code up when I was nine. No one

has figured it out so I've never had to change it. It spells home if you take A as 1. B as 2 and so on."

"You're a very clever woman, Arizona Summers. I'm sorry I ever underestimated you."

I grinned at him. "You should be."

CHAPTER THIRTY-ONE

James avoided me for the next two days. I tried to treat him as normally as I could. I hoped for an explanation but never received one.

On Friday night I had to talk to him, or drag out pots and pans and cook what I wanted myself. "Keith and I want to go to a house warming tomorrow night. Can you think of some food we could take to make the other guests ooh and ah?"

He didn't look me straight in the eye. Instead he walked to his desk in the corner and took out a note pad. I'd never seen him write anything down including new recipes.

If he was indeed a criminal, he was a poor one. Rule number one of not getting caught. Don't change your routine. "I can make stuffed mushrooms with asparagus. They are to die for."

Not a good choice of words, I thought. "Great.

We're leaving at seven. Can you put them in a warmer? The party's on the north side and we're going to walk."

The next evening I stopped by the kitchen to pick up the food and went outside to meet Keith. He had his hand on the door pull when I started to open it. "Good timing." He leaned over to smell the package I carried. "I don't know what it is, but it smells wonderful. If I had any knowledge of food I would try to guess. Want me to carry it?"

"Sure, I'll let you be a gentleman any day of the week. I haven't seen you around much, any news on James and his past?"

"No, not really."

I glanced up at a crystal clear sky. A full moon helped reflect the entire lake back at us as if it hovered under the water and we'd have to go down to the bottom and look up to see it. I stopped for a moment.

Nutmeg ran down to the lake's edge and got a drink. It distorted the image and ruined the glaze on top of the water.

"Arizona Summers, I believe you're a romantic."

I looked away from the water and straight into his eyes. "Maybe a little, I'll admit, if I didn't have to live here for business, I would still choose Moonstone Lake. I'd love to have a home with lake access."

"Why don't you move out of your apartment and buy a little house. There are two or three more on the east side."

We began to walk again. "Because of Mother, She's a young eighty, but she's set in her ways. Her great grandmother bought the Monroe Hotel, bought the nearest building to the restaurant and had it attached. They were ten inches apart. She hired an architect who worked out a way to take up the space with a fire wall.

"The hotel had three more buildings, and a quaint office. It housed twenty people when full. A Summers has lived in the building for one hundred and twenty-five years.

"The Farber family bought it thirty years ago and named it Granny's Bed and Breakfast. I don't know who owned it before them." I laughed. "You didn't ask me about it did you?"

He put his free arm on my waist. When he touched me I flinched. A tiny jolt of excitement traveled through me, I shivered. He glanced my way, totally unaware or un-phased. "It's interesting. The entire town is amazing. I hope I get to live here long enough to explore every inch of it. Jim and Mary Farber are great folks. They kept giving me weekly rates even though I stayed by the day."

I playfully bumped into him with my hip. "Did it occur to you it's because you're Chief of Police. Everyone wants a friend in your position."

"Ouch. I thought you and everyone else liked me for my sparkling personality."

I stopped in front of Roger Freedman's house. "Are you ready to go on a fact finding mission?"

"I'm ready. I should have told you this before we got this far, but I called him and asked him to come in Monday morning and make a statement about his wife and what he knew about her other life. I don't believe he'll be happy to see me."

I rang the doorbell. "You couldn't have waited until tomorrow? Guess he'll have to get over it."

"Arizona, look at this from my side. Would you want a cop to call you on Sunday and tell you to come down to the station?"

I didn't answer, but my thought was, I wouldn't want to be called in any day.

People laughed and talked. The sound floated toward us from the back yard. We followed the sidewalk and walked into the yard through a privacy gate.

Roger saw us and came over. "What are you doing here?" Two of his guests looked to see who we were. His attitude and tone changed. "Come in, this is a surprise."

Keith handed him the dish. "Sorry we didn't know you were having a get together. We dropped by to bring you a house warming dish and welcome you to your new home."

He made a grand gesture to make us welcome in front of his neighbors. He introduced us to his other guests who would soon be Keith's neighbors. I recognized most and knew the names of some.

No one knew Keith.

In all honesty, no one had reason to know the Chief of Police unless they had a need for a cop. One man stepped forward and held out his hand. "I'm Stan Fallon. This is my wife Eve. We'll be your next door neighbors on the north." He looked through the crowd until he saw the couple he wanted. "Jane, Mac, come over and meet the new comers to the street."

Enthusiasm eked out of the guy. "These are the folks who bought the house between us. Jane and

Mac Adamson, this is Keith Wesley, our new Police Chief, and his lovely wife Arizona."

Roger did a double take. "You two are married? You're moving in down the street?"

I stood, amused, and waited to hear what Keith had to say. "No, Arizona and I are friends. We aren't even dating, much less engaged or married. And yes, I bought the white house with red shutters down the street. Six houses down to be exact."

No one listened. He might as well have talked to a fence post.

Stan spoke up again. "Eve and I are thrilled about the renovations you've made on the outside. We would love to see what you've done to the inside once you're settled."

Keith smiled at his new neighbors. "I'll have a little open house when it's done. I just moved in yesterday. Right now all I have is a bed, chair, television, and a coffee pot."

Keith and I neither one were conversational whizzes. His new friends wandered off to talk to other guests. The folks at the party had most likely known one another for years.

It didn't take a genius to see Roger had enough of us. He expertly moved us toward the gate as he talked. "Thanks for coming. I'll bring the dish and carrier back to the café." He opened the gate and all but pushed us out.

Nutmeg waited outside the back gate and joined us. "Listen."

Keith looked at me. "I don't hear a sound."

I gave him a gentle push. "Exactly, want to set on the dock and listen to the quiet for a few minutes?"

"I thought maybe you would like to see my house. My real estate agent says it's charming."

"Sure, I'd love to see your chair, coffee pot, and bed." Thank goodness he didn't turn my way. When I realized what I said, I tingled from my head to my toes, with a momentary stop on the way down.

He grinned as he turned the key in the lock and swung the door open for me to see his new abode. I stepped in. Nutmeg sat on the porch. "Come on in, girl. Dogs are welcome here. Well maybe not all dogs, but certainly you." The dog scampered in and lay next to the only chair in the room.

I walked around quietly from room to room. It was small yet had all kinds of extras. They made it seem bigger than it was.

"You don't have much to say. I just knew you would love it."

I turned to him and put my hand on his chest. "I do love it. I might even be a bit jealous. Your taste of colors is spot on. Is that better?"

He put his arm across my shoulder and prepared to show me the improvements he'd made. "First, I had the wall taken out between the living room, dining room, and kitchen to make one gigantic space. Those beams on the ceiling are to hold the roof up and for looks.

"I had the contractor take out a pantry in the kitchen to enlarge the bathroom. I wanted to have a soaker tub. I know. You don't know any other men who like bubble baths, but I do. You're awfully quiet."

I shrugged away from his arm. "I was taking it all in. You have a good eye for detail. How did you end up in Moonstone Lake with no family and no personal possessions?"

His face clouded over with a horrible sadness. I could see it in his eyes as it filled the room. "That's a story for another day. Let's sit on the pier and listen to the silence you're so fond of."

I had broken his happy-go-lucky mood. He lost interest in showing me the house. We walked without talking until we arrived at Moonstone Lake Café Dock, behind the restaurant. He took my hand and helped me step up onto it. We had a wooden bench attached to the very end. We sat and listened.

Nutmeg had been lying down and moved over near me to rest her head on my feet. She sat up and looked to the top path. Keith and I both turned to see what had her interest. The shadow of a person who stood half hidden by a tree stared back at us.

Keith whispered, "Turn around, act as though you didn't see anything."

I did as he said. A minute later when I looked back, the person was gone.

He reached in his pocket and took out his phone. "Car 12, what's your position? Okay, drive by Pier 16 on the south side of the lake. This is information only. Tell me who and what you see. 10-4."

"What are you doing?"

"Deputy Marshall is parked in the lot at The Sunshine Hotel. He'll drive by this area a few times, radio back and share what he sees with us."

"Do you think it's necessary?"

"It could be. Your dog got up, came to your side and alerted you something was amiss. After observing Nutmeg, I believe she would not have done it if she thought you were safe."

I hugged my dog with all my might. "I don't know where you came from Nutmeg, but please don't ever leave."

Keith laughed. "I don't think anyone could pry that dog away from you. Before we go, I need to ask a couple of questions about James. When did he come to work for your family?"

"About two years ago."

"Do you remember anyone saying where he came from or anything about a wife, girlfriend, home town, or school, anything I can use to start an investigation?"

"His diploma hangs on the wall at the restaurant. It says clearly what culinary school he attended, and when he graduated."

"I didn't see it when we took all of the pictures the other night."

"It isn't in the kitchen. It's behind Sandra and the cashier's station. My college diploma, Sandra's, Mother's, Lewis' and James' along with all the awards for excellence and most popular restaurant certificates we've received over the years. It's getting pretty crowded."

He stood and reached down to help me stand. "Do you really think James' is a bad man?"

"I have no idea. We still have a lot of unknowns. It would be easier had the Freedman's lived in town and were part of the community. We could have watched them. But it is what it is."

We walked home in silence. I had my thoughts and I guess he had his. He said goodnight and told me to call when I got in my room. I started to leave when his phone rang. "Hi Marshall, what'd you see, anything? Really, that many people out tonight huh?" He looked at me and grinned. "They must all have been listening to the stillness. Yes, it is amazing. Be safe out there. 10-4."

"What did he see?"

"Dozens of couples walked along the Boardwalk the upper and lower paths. Others sat on docks and cooled their feet in the water. No one looked suspicious or dangerous."

"My grandmother made me sit in the quiet for ten minutes every day. She said someone tried to talk to us and I could only hear the voice if I sat still and listened. She said the voice would come from inside me.

"I told her I didn't hear a voice and no one talked to me. She said the thoughts and ideas I had come out of the silence. Don't laugh, but if I don't follow her guidance, my ears ring and I get nervous. She said there was no other path to know your real self."

He stared at me for a long moment, reached up and touched my cheek, took my hand and kissed the back of it. "Don't forget to call as soon as you're locked in your room."

CHAPTER THIRTY-TWO

I called Keith's phone as soon as Nutmeg and I were safe in the apartment. Last time I called we chatted about the case, our favorite foods, and general nonsense. This time he hung up with a *sleep well,* nothing else.

I couldn't imagine why his mood and temperament had changed so quickly. Obviously he wasn't ready to share whatever happened to him before he got to Moonstone Lake. I wasn't one to push. When he was ready, I would listen.

I hadn't been home two minutes when someone knocked on my door. For the first time, knowing it could be one of three people didn't thrill me.

I had never used the security hole in the door. There had to be a first time. I leaned down a slight bit, closed one eye and peered out. Aunt Sandy stood on the other side. I opened the door. "Hi, this is a surprise."

She plopped down on the love seat in the living room. "It shouldn't be. Before you got a dog and a boyfriend, you stopped by to visit and discuss the problems of the world. Now if I want to see you, I have to trip you."

"That's a little much, don't you think? You didn't trip me now and here we are in the same place."

She laughed. Good, I didn't ever want to be on the outs with my Aunt. From the first day I arrived at the lake, Sandy became my best buddy. My mother wasn't much of a nurturer.

I sat in a chair across from her. "Do I have to tell you he isn't my boyfriend?"

"If you did, what would I tease you about? Have any wine over here, or maybe a snack? I know you're a junk food junky, what do you have and where do you keep it?"

We walked into the kitchen one in front of the other. I opened the fridge to see if I had any wine. "I haven't been to the store lately. How about a glass of water or I have pop in here. This time I bought orange and grape."

"I'll take grape; I didn't know they still made it."

"The snacks are in the cabinet. Want me to read them off or do you want to come look yourself?"

"Surprise me; I'm going back to my comfortable chair."

I put moon pies, Oreos, Pop tarts, and cupcakes in a basket, took it in and sat it on the coffee table. "Don't blame me for your waist line if you eat some of that." I sat my orange pop on the table and grabbed four Oreos from the package. You didn't tell me what

Keith decided to do about the glove."

"He took pictures of everything. Rolled the glove back in the paper bag and we put everything back where it was before we disturbed it.

"Do you know where James worked before he came here? I remember the day we hired him... It's been almost two years. He's come a long way with me, soft spoken, young, strong and willing to do anything."

Sandy picked through the bowl and decided on a cinnamon pop tart. "He really showed his skills last year when Lewis had to have his appendix removed. James ran the kitchen smoothly and flawlessly. I feel guilty doubting him. Until the glove incident, he had never done anything out of the ordinary."

I downed the rest of my Orange Crush. "Yes, but as I look back, we took him without references. We bought his story about the fire in Chicago and he couldn't produce his certificate until it came from France. He told us he had nothing and I talked Mom into letting him live in the empty apartment until he got on his feet. Were we fools?"

Sandy reached over for another snack. "When his diploma came, it was impressive. A French culinary degree is an accomplishment?"

"I've been going over his entire time here. Do you think it's odd he doesn't have friends, and a good-looking guy like him never goes on a date? And he took off the other day to attend a funeral. He skirted the question when I asked him who died."

"Oh, Arizona, How do we know he doesn't have friends or a girl friend? I think he's just private. Private is not a crime."

"I understand what you're saying, but remember, he could be a bad man running from the bad things he did. If you were a true French chef, would you work as second in command at a diner on a lake in the middle of nowhere? Maybe I have been trying to solve too many murders. I can't help but wonder if he's in witness protection or has a record."

She came over and gave me a big hug. "I miss our little talks, but this time you have really messed up."

"Is it Mom? Was I supposed to do something and I didn't?"

"Honestly my dear niece. This time it is you. Didn't you think Emma and I would hear about the new buffet bar, the new floors, and paint?

"While you have been out pretending to be Miss Marple, everyone in the place has been guessing colors, and discussing the new arrangement. Meanwhile, my sister and I can't join in because we don't know a thing about it.

"As your mother says, *we are not going to ask anyone anything and have them realize we have been left out of the loop*. My feelings might be a little hurt, but your mother is devastated. She is of a mindset that it would be better if she weren't around at all, and this all on top of not being able to borrow money for her friends, which you also forgot to take care of."

"Oh geez, I forgot all about both of those projects. James and Lewis measured and ordered the new equipment, the workmen came to measure, and I didn't tell either of you. I don't have an excuse. I was horrible and thoughtless and I know it. Let's go up and talk to Mother right now."

"No. You're on your own on this one. I don't want

her to know I told you. She has a calendar by her chair and each day you don't share it with her or ask her opinion, she makes a big red X on it.

"I have tried never to tell you what to do, but I'm telling you now. Go talk to your mom before the sun sets on another day."

I looked out the window. With the time change it got dark at five p.m. It was after eight now. You're right, I'm on my way."

"Have a little respect for her feelings and leave Nutmeg outside."

"No. Where I go, she goes. In case James isn't the man we want him to be, I need my dog to protect me. James will be right next door when I go to her apartment."

Sandy finished her drink and snack, put the can in the trash and the basket on the table. She came over to me and offered another big hug. I took it readily. "I'll fill you in on everything in the morning after I take Mom's friends out for coffee."

She kissed me on the forehead and left.

I put the plans, color swatches, floor samples, and lists of food choices in a large tote and headed downstairs to Mother's apartment. I took Nutmeg with me. When I knocked on the door I heard. "Sandy, I was expecting you. I made fudge today."

"What kind," I asked through the closed door.

She opened the door. "Arizona. Is that you?"

"Yes Mom, it's me and the dog."

"It's about time, Come in."

"Can the dog come in?"

"Of course, right now, she's more welcome than you."

What could I say? She was right. For forty-five years she practically lived in the café. Five years she worked with grandma to learn the ropes, thirty years she ran it by herself and made a larger profit every year, the last five years, she taught me all she could. She made all the chores seem easy, but they were not. "Hi mom, sorry I'm just now getting here with the plans for the remodel. I've been busy. Actually Mom, I don't have any excuse. I just forgot."

She closed the door behind me and walked toward the kitchen. "I hope the bag you're carrying has everything in it I want to see. Sit down. I'm not going to flog you or make you walk the plank. Let me have a look. Have you shown this to Sandy yet?"

"No, I haven't."

"Then get out that fancy phone of yours and tell her to get down here and let's see what the new design is going to look like. Don't look at me that way. I wasn't angry, I was hurt and I'm sure Sandy is too. While we wait for your aunt, pour three glasses of the wine. It's in the refrigerator. Goodness child, then have a seat."

The evening went surprisingly well. Mom and Sandy liked the idea and made some suggestions about space and color that were helpful.

Within ten minutes of Sandy's arrival, we were laughing and joking like we did before Mom retired. I needed it. We all needed it.

I decided to take Nutmeg for a walk after we left the meeting. Keith's voice was nearly audible in my ear telling me it wasn't safe. With two suspects within a couple of miles, maybe I should have been afraid. As we left the building I figured in my head how many times I had run the same path.

If I included the twenty plus miles a week I ran in cross country for six years. I'd run over twelve thousand miles. If I took out my college days, sick days, and nasty weather days, I had run the upper path's five mile loop more than sixty-thousand miles.

It was difficult to be scared when you know a path as well as I knew that one.

I put on my running shoes, took Nutmegs lead off of her and away we went. No matter how other people categorized jogging, it relaxed me and calmed my soul. It was after midnight when I ran the first portion and made the turn to head home.

I smiled when I ran past Keith's nautical home and grimaced when I got to Roger Freedman's. The café' was in view when I lost my balance and fell flat on my face. It happened too quickly for me to prepare.

Where had Nutmeg gone? I didn't hear her bark, the last memory I had before I passed out was a whisper, *Stay out of this investigation. Go back to cooking"*.

Where was my dog?

The first thought I had when I opened my eyes was of Nutmeg. Had someone hurt her?

I felt her furry paw on my arm. I couldn't move enough to see if she was hurt. Tears ran down my face and hit the pavement. My dog stood over me and licked my face.

Sirens blared in the distance. Someone stood over me. I heard a voice say, "No don't move her. Wait for the ambulance. Look, the dog is bleeding."

Then Nutmeg growled. It was a warning, a mean

growl *I'm going to bite if you make another move.*

"Is my dog hurt?" Did I think it or say it. No one answered so I tried to talk louder. "Is my dog hurt?"

I heard a voice I recognized as Keith's. He lay on the path beside me and looked at my face. "Can you feel your arms and legs?"

The answer to my question was the only thing I cared about at the moment. "Is my dog hurt?"

"No, no she's not. From the looks of things around here, I'd say someone ran a fishing line from a tree on one side of the trail to a tree on the other side. It won't be difficult to find out who did this. Nutmeg has a piece of torn clothing next to her. She's guarding it. Do you have enough strength to have her give it to me?"

"Nutmeg, come. Give your trophy to Keith. He's a good guy."

It took all the strength I had and I knew I couldn't say or do another thing.

Later, I don't know how much later I awoke in a room with lights so bright I had to close my eyes.

I saw Mother. "Are you better?"

"Yes, help me sit up. I didn't see the string. It knocked the breath out of me. The way it hurts now I believe it will be sore for a while."

I heard someone say. "Don't sit up quite yet. It's time for all of you to go. I need to examine Ms. Summers. I'll come out as soon as I can to give you an update on her condition."

It became quiet again." I'm Dr. McManus, the emergency doctor on call this evening. He poked and prodded. "Does it hurt? Can you feel this? Can you see out of your left eye? Raise your right arm until it hits my hand. Now the left, let's try it with your right leg, now the left."

I heard Keith. It sounded like his voice came from a large barrel full of water. "Hi Ary, the doctor says you're fine, he's talking to your mom. You're going to have a black eye and both wrists are going to hurt. You ran into that fishing line hard enough to cut your right leg. All in all, you're okay. Can you tell me what happened?"

"I'm not certain. I was running and a second later I was on the ground. Where's Nutmeg?"

"Everyone was upset because she had blood on her. She took a pretty good bite out of someone. I was excited thinking all we needed was a DNA sample and we'd have the assailant and maybe the murderer. Before I could get a sample your dog went into the lake and gave herself a bath. There wasn't a useable sample left on her."

"Through this foggy brain of mine I thought I heard someone say Nutmeg bit whoever it was. Can't you get your DNA from the piece of cloth she has?"

He put his hand in mine and I squeezed it. "I feel like I was hit by a truck. I'm getting much too old to fall. When can I go home?"

"The doctor's getting your orders together and then he'll be in to talk with you."

"Where's Nutmeg?"

"She is just inside the emergency room door. They said she could stay there if she didn't roam around."

I smiled. "Bring that tray over here, will you? I feel like my eye takes up my entire face."

He pushed it to me and opened the lid. "My

goodness, I must have hit right eye first. What a mess."

The doctor came in, "Yes it is. You don't have any permanent damage, but as your eye gets well, it will turn every color in the rainbow. You need someone to stay with you tonight. You shouldn't sleep more than two hour stretches in case you have a concussion. I don't think so, but better safe than sorry.

"I don't know if you are a pain pill taker or not, but I suggest you take two of these every four hours through tomorrow. The nurse will be in with your discharge papers and you're free to go."

"Tell me what happened; everything you can remember."

"I could see the apartment building and challenged Nutmeg to a race. Next thing I knew I was on the ground. At first I thought it was someone who Nutmeg knew because she didn't bark, most likely she was too busy biting to bark."

"Did you see or hear anything?"

"Yes, someone told me to stop the investigation. He said to go back to cooking, what time is it?"

He looked at his phone. "3:30, did the voice sound familiar?"

"No, he said it so softly I had to think a minute to realize what he said. I wish that nurse would hurry up. I need to get some sleep. It's my turn to go in early."

"No you don't. Your Aunt Sandy and your mother are going to handle it."

"But Keith, it's Sunday. I don't know if they can handle it."

"They both said the same thing. Sundays are the easiest. Clear the tables keep the drinks full and smile at the customers."

"That sounds like something Mom would say."

"Bingo."

The nurse with the forms showed up a little later and off we went. Nutmeg was near the police cruiser when I got in. I didn't know who was happiest, me or her.

She whined and whined. I hugged her. "Oh baby," I told her. "It's not your fault. I hear you got a piece of him."

She barked three times, turned in circles, and, wagged her tail."

Keith rested his hand on the gun rack between us. "I have some news for you. Going on my assumption that Roger Freedman or your Chef James is a murderer, I went to visit them to see if either one had a recent dog bite."

It took him so long to go on I yelled, "what, what?"

"It seems James had to leave because his father is gravely ill. He told Lewis he would be back as soon as he could. He'll call and keep you posted."

"You mean James did this to me?"

"Oh, the story gets better than that. Roger Freedman went to settle some business in Boston. He left late last night. No one knows when he'll return either."

I leaned forward and turned toward him. "You mean to tell me the only two viable suspects we have in Ruth Freedman's murder and my assault left town?"

"Yes, that's exactly what I'm telling you. And I checked every flight from the two local airports and no one by either of those names booked a flight. I checked the two closest big airports. No luck."

I put my hand over my mouth. "What are the chances they're in this together?"

"I doubt they are. By the way I took the liberty of changing the codes on your front apartment door, and the café' alarms. I also had a dead bolt put on James' apartment door and the front and back doors at Roger's house."

"Can you do that?"

"I gave it a lot of thought. I would rather beg forgiveness than put you or anyone else in danger."

"What are you going to do?"

"After I get you and Nutmeg home and safely tucked in, I am going to take a picture of James' culinary degree and see if I can track him back to an old address. See if I can find out anything about him. I'll be back to wake you up in two hours."

I wasn't sure if it was the excitement of what I had just heard, the car ride, or my injuries but I slumped against the door and fought not to faint.

Keith turned the wheels toward the sidewalk, turned on his bubble lights and ran to my side of the car. "Are you sick?"

"Most likely the entire event has worn me down. I'm ready for a nap. Am I supposed to do anything for my eye? It throbs and feels like it takes up more of my face than it did a while ago. All I can say is, ouch."

"The hospital sent an ice bag, but it needs to go in the freezer before it's any good. Great planning, huh."

I tried to smile but I just couldn't.

We rode the rest of the way in silence. Keith took me upstairs and went back down to tell Sandy and Mom I was home. He took Nutmeg for a walk. "Will you be okay until I can get back? Marshall will be out front. If James comes home, we'll intercept him. I have another car in front of Roger's house. Right now it's a waiting game."

"A waiting game." I repeated.

CHAPTER THIRTY-THREE

I came out of a fog. Someone tried to sit me up. I slapped the hand away.

"Whoa, Ary, It's me, Keith. The doctor said to wake you up every two hours. Maybe you should sit in a chair while I find a dry blanket."

"Why is my blanket wet?"

"I'm not a doctor but I'd say you're sweaty from the pain. "I've got a pain pill for you."

I sat and watched him take my wet blanket off the bed and replace it with another. He sat on the edge of the bed. "Are you awake enough to hear some bizarre news?"

"Sure, maybe it'll make me feel better."

"I took a picture of James' diploma, and researched it. James Aloysisus Coutute. It says he graduated from Meilleur Cuiseur D'oeufs, Eze, France, June 15, 2006."

"I've seen it. It's been on the wall the last year and a half. He said the original burned in a fire. The school sent him a new one."

"There hasn't been a James Aloysisus Countute in the United States since 1872, and he died of dysentery at age fifty. James seems to have appeared as him for the first time three years ago. There is nothing before then. We looked up his social security number. It belonged to a child named Ryan Dubois who died when he was six.

"Now, for the bigger news, Meilleur Cuiseur D'ocefus is not a school of any kind. It translates to *Best Egg Cooker*. I bet he laughed about it every day."

"It's hard for me to accept. He's such a nice guy. He works every day, never complains, he's soft spoken. Maybe there's a reasonable explanation."

"I don't know. I'm waiting for a judge to sign a search warrant so I can get into his apartment for some DNA and fingerprint samples. DNA identification takes forever but we should be able to get fingerprints. I can run them through CODES.

"Time for you to go back to bed, I'll get you some water, if you need the restroom, I'm sure you can find it."

"Keith, I want to go with you when you search James' room."

"You can go in, but I have a CSI crew on its way. They'll go in first and check out everything. Once they are done, I'll come get you. The thing is, I believe James will come back with a story about his dad. He had no reason to leave except for the bite Nutmeg left on him somewhere. We need to get in, get what we need and get out without touching things. I'll take pictures I can blow up later and see what I can find that way. Go back to sleep. I'll wake you in a couple of hours."

"Can you take Nutmeg out while you're here?"

"I did that before I woke you up, didn't I Nutmeg?"

"I'll rest, but I won't be able to sleep knowing what's going on."

Nutmeg crawled in bed with me. I turned toward her. It's the last thing I remember until Mother came in. "Arizona, time to sit up again. Keith's busy and asked me to take care of you."

I was awake, as soon as it sunk into my spinning brain what Keith was up to. "Is he downstairs at James' apartment?"

"No honey. He just left. He said to tell you he'll be back soon. And why on earth would he be in James' apartment. I think you got hit harder than we thought.

"I brought soup. Do I need to feed it to you, do you want a spoon, or would you rather drink it?"

"I'll drink it. I smelled it when you came in: chicken noodle. How is it going downstairs?"

"It's four o'clock. We're closed and cleaned. Sandy and I helped Lewis and the crew in the kitchen. He's really swamped without James."

"Has Lewis said anything about James?"

"No, only that he hopes his dad's doing better. Have you checked your phone to see if he has tried to contact you?"

"No, but I will after I take a shower. I feel yucky."

"You've got quite a shiner."

Mom left. As much as I wanted to take a shower, I couldn't. I wanted to be ready to go inside our missing chef's apartment. I fell asleep again with murder, floating bodies, and weddings on my mind.

When I awoke some time later, it was dark. I had lost an entire day. Keith sat dozing in a chair with his feet on the window sill. He looked exhausted. I wanted to find out what happened downstairs but he looked so peaceful it could wait.

I couldn't stand myself any longer; I grabbed some clean clothes and headed for the shower. My balance wasn't as good as I thought it should be. I attributed it to too much sleep. I had to keep one hand on the tub or hold on to the shower curtain so as not to fall.

When he opened his sleepy eyes he asked, "Hi, everything okay?"

"I think so. My face throbs but otherwise I'm ready to get going. I need something cold to drink."

I went into the kitchen. When I got to the icebox I turned around, he was so close I could smell his sweet breath. He took a step back. "Sorry, got a cold beer in there?"

"No. You won't like what I have. Last time I was at the store, I craved things from when I was a kid. I bought Orange Crush and Grape soda."

"I'll have a grape. We can sit in the living room and I'll tell you what I know."

"Start talking, is it witness protection?"

"James' real name is Travis Hall. He was born in San Francisco on October 20, 1983. He owned a catering company in Boston, but lost the business. We think he'll be back to work as soon as the wound heals. How many people at the restaurant know it was James who caused you to fall and Nutmeg bit him?"

"Only three of us; me, you, and Sandy and she wouldn't tell a soul."

"What did you tell your Mom when she came to the hospital?"

"I tripped over a rock and fell on my face."

"Good job. Right now, that's all the information we have. I wanted to come back here in case you had told your mother. I was going to have a talk with her. Marshall's running the name Travis Hall through the Division of Motor Vehicles, military records, culinary schools, department of corrections and FBI. When James comes back, you and your aunt are going to have to become great actresses."

My phone rang. It was James. I turned it on speaker. *"Hello."*

James – *"You sound chipper. Things have been sad around here."*

Me- *"How's your father?"*

James- *"He passed away last night. Sorry I haven't kept in touch more, but sitting vigil is hard work."*

Me – *"I'm so sorry. How is your family taking it?"*

James- *"There is only me. That's why I thought it was my place to stay by his side. The funeral is Thursday and I have a few papers to sign. I should be back no later than Saturday. Are you working Lewis to death?"*

Me. *"Not too bad. Lewis took over your spot and Mother has been making all the desserts. She is exhausted, but I think she likes it. James, if you give me the address of the funeral home and your dad's name we'll send flowers."*

James. *"It's not necessary. I'll see you Saturday. Tell everyone hi for me."*

Me- *"Would you like me to have someone…"*

I looked at the face of the phone. "He hung up."

Keith grinned. "You were great, academy award performance."

"It's one thing to talk to him on the phone, but until I find out why he wanted to hurt me, it will be difficult to treat him as though nothing happened."

He took my hand. "Want to go for a walk? You've been in bed nearly twenty-four hours straight. The fresh air might do you some good. It's a beautiful warm night. Maybe it will help you figure out how to handle James."

He had to help me tie my shoes. When I bent over my eye tried to fall out. I hadn't expected it to hurt so bad. I changed my focus to the sweet, damp, warm air around me and pushed the pain away. "You're right about the night air. It feels like we skipped spring and went right on to summer."

We strolled along the sidewalk and followed it around the restaurant and down to the pier. I sat. Nutmeg jumped up and sat beside me. Keith was on the opposite end. He leaned forward around the dog. "I think there's something between us."

I laughed and ask Nutmeg to get down. "How long will you let the charade go on with James before you confront him? I'm not comfortable with any of it. What if circumstances happen to put me and James alone together?"

"I'll try to see it doesn't happen. Do you have a

gun?"

"Aunt Sandra and I went to a conceal and carry class. The man said, *if you don't think you can kill another human being, you should leave now. People who pull a weapon and hesitate to use it end up the victim.* We left. I'm not sure I could end a life."

He held my hand. "I wish you had one, but the man was right. You can get hurt if you don't understand guns or if you're afraid of them. Maybe when this is over, I can help you become more at ease with a weapon."

I turned toward him. "You didn't answer my question. How long does a case like this last?"

"It depends. If all of the records come back clean, he doesn't have any warrants and we ascertain he didn't kill Ruth Freedman, we'll charge him with assault.

"He ordered a fake diploma, changed his name and has no past. None of it is a good sign. I can't think of one reason except Witness Protection and they wouldn't give him a Mickey Mouse diploma and send him out into the real world."

I raised the hand he had his on top of and pointed at the sky. "Look, a shooting star. There's another one. We must be having a meteor shower."

We sat and watched in silence a few minutes before he said, "You know, we haven't ruled out Roger Freedman as the person who killed his wife or maybe the two men together. We're a little bit further along than we were before. He left because a father no one knew he had got sick and died. He has no pictures, mementos or books in his apartment. What does he do in there night after night?

"I'd bet my paycheck it was either Roger or James. Did I tell you the FBI tracked Roger to Chicago, not Boston where he said he was going? He made a trip to the bank where Ruth had stashed the money. Since the name on the account was bogus and so were the beneficiaries, he signed off saying he had nothing to do with it and he wasn't heir to it. The Foundation's money was returned.

"The report the FBI sent listed Dillon as next in line to run the Foundation. He said no way. He signed it over to the Board of Directors with the stipulation they all had to decide on the recipients and it would take at least two signatures to sign a check."

"Wise man." I said.

CHAPTER THIRTY-FOUR

I worked a half day. I needed a little more rest before I went back to my regular schedule. Mother smiled and kept working but I noticed she took more breaks.

One of Lewis' jobs, once he had the desserts perfected, was to keep the buffet full as people came and went.

The next day I took over for Mom and had her quit once she and Lewis had the baking taken care of. Two more days and James would be back. My stomach churned and the hair stood up on the back of my neck each time I thought about him. At night I dreamed more than once he held my head under water and I couldn't get away.

I wanted him to come back and then I didn't. It frosted me he had a diploma that made fun of us. I wanted the truth, but I didn't want to get hurt like Ruth Freedman to find out.

On the other hand Roger Freedman had slipped into life in Moonstone Lake. He checked in with Keith when he returned to town and proved he didn't have a scratch on him. Honestly, I hoped he stayed off the suspect list. After I got to know him, it was difficult not to like him.

I was about to lock the front door when Keith pushed on the other side. He waved some papers in the air. "I've got news."

"You know I'm excited to hear it, but since we are short-handed, I need to stay here and help. Can you entertain yourself for an hour?"

"Sure, I'll take Nutmeg for a run."

I didn't have to say a word to the dog. She crawled from under the podium, wagged her tail, and went happily with Keith. I wasn't sure how I felt about it.

By the time they got back, I was seated on the bench in front of the apartment waiting for them. TLC Handyman's truck was parked on the street and the front door of the building was propped open.

Did I let Keith take too many liberties with my home?

He showed up a minute later so I asked him. "Why is the door propped open? You know I haven't been feeling very safe lately?"

"Marshall's in there with the handyman. Remember, I put a pad lock on James' door. I needed to have it removed and the door redone so he wouldn't notice. I should have told you about it."

"Okay."

"Hey don't get glum. I have news for you about Travis Hall. At age two, the Halls moved from St. Louis to Boston. He spent four years in the Army as a cook. There's no record of him having graduated from any culinary school. Eight years ago he opened a catering business, *Special Occasion Catering* in Boston. Two and a half years ago, he closed it abruptly and he was never seen again. He resurfaced here as James Couture and ends up working at the café, no arrests, warrants, or dirty deeds. At least nothing obvious showed up on a standard fact finding mission."

I hugged Nutmeg who sat panting by my leg. "Did you give her any water?"

"I forgot, but I have some in the car. Be right back. He brought a plastic ice cream container, took the lid off and sat it down for the dog." He looked at me. "I keep this in the car now."

The workman came out of the house in front of Marshall. Keith locked the door and came back to the bench. "There could be a connection between the Freedman's and James. They both lived in Boston at the same time. Travis had a catering company. We both know how Ruth treated everyone she came in contact with. Maybe they knew one another. Maybe she hired him to do something."

"Did you ever question Roger?"

"No, I was going to interview him the Monday after you fell. He left without notifying me. I didn't specify a time. I'll make sure he shows up as soon as he gets back into town."

"I need to go in. My face still aches and until James comes back, I'll have to chip in and help with the cooking and cleaning."

"Until we get this case straightened out, you'll see a lot of me. Right now, duty calls. The FBI put Roger

Freedman on a plane in Chicago after he signed the papers. Officer Malloy is at the airport to pick him up. They should be back at the office in about fifteen minutes."

"If I stay out of sight can I go along and listen in. I promise I won't make a sound or tell a soul."

He stood still and looked at me with a strange look. "Are you the same Arizona who told me her face hurt and she needed to go to bed? Are you sure you're up to it?"

"I'm sure. I would be pacing the floor waiting for you to call and tell me what happened. You aren't a good one to put in all of the facts. This way I know I won't miss anything."

Nutmeg, who had been asleep, walked over in front of Keith and barked twice. "Okay, but not a word. My plan was to talk to him in my office but I could use an interrogation room. We'd better get going. I want you neatly tucked out of the way before he arrives."

The interrogation room had a two way mirror. Marshall put a chair near the window for me to sit in and asked if I was comfortable. I was so excited to be able to listen to Roger I could have sat on tacks and been fine.

Some minutes later Keith and Roger walked into the room on the other side of the mirror. The chief walked around and sat with his back to me which gave Roger the seat facing me. "Mr. Freedman, I want to thank you for coming in with Officer Malloy."

Roger reached into one sports coat sleeve and pulled his shirt sleeve down and repeated it on the other side. "I got the feeling I didn't have a choice."

"If you remember, we were supposed to have this little meeting last Monday. I didn't want to miss you again."

I couldn't read Roger's face, but he didn't answer.

"I'm going to turn on this camera and tape recorder just to make sure we both remember the same things about this conversation."

"Chief, are you going to read me my rights?"

"No sir, not unless you want me to. I'm not charging you with anything. Mainly I want to talk about your wife. And a few general questions to help with the investigation."

"Okay, let's get started. It's been a long week."

"Well then, where did you live in Boston?"

"In Brookline."

"Did you ever meet a man by the name of Travis Hall?"

"Not that I can remember. We lived there for thirty years, but the name doesn't sound familiar."

"Tell me about your wife. Did you two have any marital problems?"

"My wife was a wonderful woman until Dillon came along. Then she made him her life's work. As he grew up she made sure he was the standout in all he did. I told her how hard it was on the boy but she wouldn't listen."

"Did she revert back to her old ways after he grew up?"

"I hate to say much more, I'm making it seem more and more like I murdered her, and I didn't."

"I'm not taking it that way, Mr. Freedman."

"Good. I have been thinking a lot about Ruth since

her death and it feels good to get it out. When Dillon was in the ninth grade, Ruth's father died and she became Executive Director of his Foundation and caretaker of eight-hundred-and fifty million dollars.

"She was supposed to feed the poor and winterize their homes, get air conditioning for the elderly and to feed as many people as possible. She acted like that money was hers and she made it horrible for the people she was supposed to be helping. The forms were longer, the basic salaries to qualify for assistance became higher. She wouldn't listen to reason. The charity went from a four A to a B.

"I didn't, however, know she was a thief. We're not hurting for money. My father was Mathew Freedman of Freedman Steel. I inherited enough for any ten families. She didn't need to steal. When I found out it went on for years, and she never touched any of the money, has to say something for her mental state. Why someone would amass a fortune, put it in a bank a thousand miles away in the names of some book characters is beyond me. I've had it on my mind since she passed. I feel bad for the people who were supposed to get the money.

"Let me tell you one more thing and then I don't believe you'll have to ask me any more questions. I did not kill my wife. I don't miss Ruth. I haven't missed her one minute since she died. She was mean, petty and rude. She hurt the feelings of every person she came in contact with. Chief, I don't think you can arrest me for not loving or respecting my wife. May I go now?"

Keith didn't move. Roger Freedman looked down at his hands. It was eerily quiet in there. I don't know how he did it but Keith must have called Randy into the room, "Officer Malloy would you please drive Mr. Freedman home?"

They shook hands before Roger left.

I waited a reasonable amount of time then left the room. Keith was alone in his office. I tapped on the glass in the door. "Can we come in?"

"I was on my way to get you."

"Sure you were."

He walked around and sat on the front edge of his desk. "Can you imagine living with someone who hates people day and night for over thirty years?

"Nutmeg and I are going home."

"No, I'll take you."

We rode home in silence.

Mom didn't show up for work the next morning. Aunt Sandy ran over to her apartment to see if she overslept. She came back and handed me a note.

Arizona, I'm taking the day off. It's something you can do when you're retired. I'm getting my hair done, a manni and a peddi and a full body massage. Everybody needs a spa day once in a while. If it perks me up, I might go shopping. Love, Mother

Aunt Sandy had a twinkle in her eyes. She put a hand on each of my shoulders and looked me straight in the eye and began to laugh. It hit me just right and I began to laugh too. We laughed until we cried. We needed it.

CHAPTER THIRTY-FIVE

"Hey Arizona." I turned around and there stood James.

I walked over and gave him a hug. When I saw him a shadow of doubt crossed my mind. How did I know he killed someone? Maybe he faked a culinary certificate because he needed a job.

A cold chill ran up my back. Yet again, maybe he did. "You're a sight for sore eyes."

He reached up and moved my head so he could get a better look at my face. "Speaking of sore eyes, what happened to you?"

"I guess some kids were trying to pull a prank. They tied a piece of fishing twine across the trail and I tripped over it. They got punished—Nutmeg bit one of them,"

He looked down at the dog. "Good job Nutmeg."

Nutmeg stood behind me and didn't go near him.

Maybe she was surer than I about who did what. "Glad you're back. Sorry about your dad."

"Thanks, Mom and Dad were in their forties when they had me. He died peacefully. That's what mattered to me."

"Why are you limping? Did you hurt your leg?"

"The nurses were nice enough to let me use their kitchen. One of them didn't realize I had boiled some water for tea. She picked it up by the hot handle and dropped it immediately. It burned me. At least I was at a hospital and didn't have to go anywhere to have it treated."

"That's a shame. It just added to everything else you had going on."

He picked up his bag and turned toward the door. "I can't get in the front door. Is it broken or did you change the codes?"

I walked over to the cashier's station to get a piece of paper. "I will write it down for you. Someone tried to rob the restaurant. I changed the security codes for the alarm and while I was at it, I went ahead and changed ours too." I wrote the numbers down for him and handed them over with a smile. "Will you be ready to work tomorrow?"

"Let me put my things away and change clothes. I'll be back in time to work the lunch and dinner shifts."

"That's great. I'll tell Lewis. He'll be thrilled."

Before I went into the kitchen, I texted the chief a message… *James is back. I was hyper friendly. He has a limp, said he burned it when a pot of hot water fell on him.*

I think he did it. Nutmeg doesn't like him anymore.

Lewis grinned when I told him James came home. "I don't know who is the happiest, me or my legs. They miss the coffee breaks we can take when there is a full crew."

My cell phone dinged I had a message. It was Keith… *A burn huh? I'll be there in about an hour for lunch.*

I had a sudden burst of energy. My doubts about whether he killed Ruth Freedman were gone. I didn't believe in coincidences. Nutmeg bit my attacker on the leg. James happened to spill hot water on his leg. Nutmeg wouldn't go near him.

Sadness overwhelmed me. I didn't want to think he had it in him to kill someone. I didn't want to think he had the mindset to hurt me.

We worked at practically a dead run all day. Amy had a dentist appointment right in the middle of the afternoon rush. I played waitress. Each time I did, it reminded me of how hard the staff worked. I had never taken the time to hire another waiter or waitress. I made a mental note not to put it off any longer.

The chief and two of his officers came in together. Randy Malone and Keith but I didn't know the third person. When I went to take their order, Randy introduced me before Keith had the chance. "Ary, this is our new patrol officer, Amanda Wade."

"Amanda, I'm so glad to meet you. The Moonstone Lake Police Department just went up two points in my book. What are you hungry for? I'd love to buy your first work lunch."

Liz Austin walked in and I excused myself to say

hi. "Hey stranger, what's new on the newsbeat?"

"If you have time, I'd love to tell you."

"Give me a minute to see if Sandra will take over for me. She just came in." It only took a minute. "Okay, I'm back. What's your news?"

"There was a young chef in Boston who catered a wedding for Mrs. Freedman. He prepared the food and cake. The entire guest list became ill. It was discovered a few days later the vanilla he used in the icing was tainted." She took a deep breath and continued. "Story is, the chef didn't know the vanilla had been recalled until the next morning. There were three hundred guests give or take a few. Very few of the people didn't eat the cake, most did. The chef gave all the money back plus a tidy sum for inconvenience. His insurance took care of the medical expenses of everyone who needed treatment.

Ruth Freedman didn't let it go. She picketed in front of the business and called the newspapers. They massacred him on her say so. The place was called Special Occasions Catering. He went bankrupt and lost his business. He sued the paper and lost."

"I'm guessing you think it has something to do with the murder."

"I do. His name was Travis Hall. Does that ring a bell with you?"

My legs buckled. I slipped into the closest booth. Liz sat on the edge of the other side. Travis Hall.

"Arizona, are you alright? Your face is white."

"Sure, I'm fine, just worn out from the busy day."

Liz had a paper in her hand. She placed it face down on the table and slid it to me. "Here is a picture of him."

The face that stared back at me was James. No more guessing. The evidence and the motive lay on the table in front of me. "Who else knows?"

"Nobody but you and me."

"Keith and I know. He did a background check using fingerprints he found in James' apartment. We didn't know he had had a run in with Ruth Freedman. I bet he freaked out when he found out the wedding was her son's. Do you have to turn the story in?"

"No. I dug it up myself. If you want me to bury it, I can."

"It's important that you do. I have things to tell you too. I have to go back to work now. I've left customers waiting as it is. I'll call you as soon as I have time."

Liz got up to leave, I stopped her. "Remember not a word to anyone until we find out what Keith wants to do. If James gets a whiff of any of this, he will run and we may never find him."

She held up her hand and extended her little finger like we did in high school. "Pinky swear."

I returned the gesture, "Pinky swear."

She turned as she reached the door. "Come over tonight. I haven't had anyone in my place since I moved to the apartment upstairs from The Hoof and Mane."

"I'll be there. Okay if I bring Nutmeg?"

"Of course, see you then." And she was gone.

I didn't get back to serve Moonstone Lake's Police. I don't know who waited on them. I knew when I had a chance to tell Keith what happened he would forgive me.

The afternoon lag arrived and I went to a booth in

the back to take a break, Sandy joined me. Matt brought us each the special. I was too excited to eat. I wanted to tell her, but I couldn't. It would be a betrayal to not tell Keith, swear Liz to secrecy and break the promise myself.

What a difference a minute makes. I looked up as Mother sashayed through the door. I tapped my Aunt's hand and motioned for her to turn around.

Mom walked to us with one hand holding her skirt out away from her body and the other up and bent at the elbow in a royalty wave. She had Lucille Ball orange hair. Her bangs were long and fell all the way down to her chin. The side opposite them was army recruit short and stood up with what I guessed was butch wax. I took a deep breath so as not to laugh. I wouldn't have looked at Sandy right then for a million dollars.

She pulled out her full snow white skirt and twirled around in a circle several times. Apparently it made her dizzy because she rested her hand on the table.

She had chosen a lavender long sleeve pull over with a plunge in the front so deep I bet with a little maneuvering I could have seen her belly button.

On her feet she sported knee high boots that laced to the top. At least they were black.

I couldn't help catching a glimpse of her new manicure including the tiger stripes.

I spoke to her first. "Looks like you had a productive day. Have you seen the color of your hair?"

Aunt Sandy kicked me under the table. "Emma, would you like to join us? Surely you're hungry after your work over—I mean makeover."

I tried to redeem myself. "I didn't say I didn't like it. I just asked if you had seen it."

"Yes, Arizona, I have. She scooted into the booth next to her sister. Someone whose hair is as red and unruly as yours should not insult the color others pick." She touched the back which was a mass of curls like you would see on a poodle. "It's called Heavenly Tangerine."

Matt walked up to the table and asked, "Miss, can I...oh Mrs. Summers, you look...different. Can I get you something?"

She stood and almost knocked him over. "No. I ate with my friends. We are going to Johnsonville to see a movie later. I intend to show off my new look." She waddled off.

Aunt Sandy looked at me. "Was it as horrible as I think it was?"

"No, three times worse. How long do you think she'll have that hair cut?"

"About six weeks if she begins to let it grow out. If she likes it, it could be years."

"Look at it this way. We nagged her to do something besides sit in her apartment all day, and she did.

CHAPTER THIRTY-SIX

I walked to Liz's apartment by myself and it gave me the willies. I had to remind myself I'd lived in the same town for twenty-six years. At age twelve, Mom let me walk all the way over to the north side when I wanted a snack, but never at night.

I had put my tennis shoes on in case I needed to run. In the back of my mind, I still had the vivid thought that Nutmeg didn't bring my assailant down. Since I was out cold, I knew there had to be more to the mishap than I knew. Even though Nutmeg had to be the world's smartest dog, she couldn't talk and tell me what happened.

My theory, I hadn't shared it with anyone, James stood somewhere in a shadow. When I tripped on the wire he had rigged, he came over. Since he was a friend, Nutmeg hung back. She thought James was there to help. Once she realized he had come to hurt me she attacked and bit him.

Different scenarios ran through my mind as to why he wanted to kill me. The most logical — he knew I suspected him in Ruth Freedman's death.

On my way over, I received a text from my favorite policeman.

I read it. *Wish I could see the, so called, burn on James' leg.*

I answered: *Maybe he had good reason to kill her, does that count for anything?*

Him: *That's a strange question. I guess my answer is, she's just as dead whether he meant to kill her or not. Gotta go, big accident on Highway 13. Talk tomorrow.*

I was glad the conversation was over. Guilt had me by the hand. I knew he told me not to go out alone until the case was solved, and I agreed.

I could smell a luscious fragrance as soon as I opened the outside door of Liz's apartment building. The narrow staircase had little flashing lights wrapped around one side of the banister from top to bottom to make it easier to navigate. A heart shaped sign on the door read *Only Those Pure of Heart Welcome Here*. Until that moment I had forgotten Liz was an accomplished painter.

She opened the door as I stepped on the top step. The interior made me gasp. She'd painted the walls with flowers, moons, and the sun, in bright colors. No one else could pull off lime green woodwork. I knew if I went home and described it to Aunt Sandy she would say it sounded bilious. She loved the word bilious.

The tiny apartment looked like something out of

Shabby Chic Magazine. My eyes were drawn to the living room and its gigantic floor to ceiling windows. She gave me the tour, a large kitchen with chickens of every kind painted around the bottom of the wall so it looked like a real barnyard. I knew if I looked at them long enough one of them would walk away. A tiny bedroom held as much charm as the rest of the apartment. Lilacs and daisies danced together on the wall above her bed. The other three walls supported pale pastel horizontal stripes with the words to the *Dance*, by Garth Brooks painted on it. A one word description for it had to be fairyland like.

I didn't have one picture on my walls. Hers didn't need any. I had to attribute my bare walls to laziness.

As the glowing mood of the space embraced me, I promised myself I'd make a trip to Mason's Fine Art down the street and find something I liked to hang on my walls. Better yet, maybe Liz would paint something for my dull living space.

"What is the fragrance, it's intoxicating?"

"It's my favorite. It's called Nag Champa. I can't take credit; it's the most popular incense in the world. What you smell is floral and Sandalwood."

"I'm in love with it."

"Would you like a glass of wine? I have red or white."

"I remember you to be a Mascoto lover so I'll take the red and hope you still favor it."

She went into the kitchen and I followed along. "I see your easel and paints in the corner of the living room. Are you painting for you or to sell?"

"There are several at Mason's. The tourists seem to like them."

"Does it matter where I sit?"

"No, everything is equally old." Nutmeg went to her for a pet. "You're such a good baby I forgot you were here. You can sit anywhere you want, pretty girl."

Nutmeg wagged her tail and lay in front of my chair. "After lunch did you dig up any more information on Travis Hall?"

"As a matter of fact, I did. Six months after Ruth Freedman ruined him, he sued her for character assassination. He lost, and moved his business to New York under a new name. All Occasion Catering.

A critic found out he was the same chef Mrs. Freedman ruined in Boston and ran the story. It said in the paper his crew quit, and no one would hire him. He sold his equipment at auction and disappeared."

I was too absorbed in her information to drink my wine. I realized I had held it up to my lips the entire time she talked. "Can you imagine how he felt when Ruth showed up here for her son's wedding?"

"From what I read, no one would cater for her in Boston. When she had a Foundation event, she had her assistant handle it. They still had to bring in a company from Vermont."

I leaned forward. "Goodness, Liz, how do you find out the personal stuff? I know it isn't written down anywhere."

"I've been doing this for a long time. I've learned who to call. Some people are talkers. I don't know anyone from the northeast. I called my people in St. Louis and Kansas City and they came through for me."

I rubbed Nutmeg's back with my foot. "I have no

idea how Keith will catch him. No one saw him around her. She didn't come to the tasting before the reception. Something else occurred to me. Roger said his wife left the same day she was killed. Do you think he knew what James did and covered for him?"

Liz held her glass in the air as a signal it was empty. I tipped mine to her and she filled them both. "I say we trap him."

I did a double take. "Sounds pretty dangerous to me, did you forget, he poisoned her first?"

"The police chief's your buddy, maybe we could bring him in on this."

"I doubt he'd go for it. He'd have a fit if he knew I walked over here by myself. I didn't tell you how I got the black eye, but we're sure James did it." I gave her an abbreviated version of what happen.

"Since he wants to hurt you, let's get him before he gets you."

"I've made up to him since he got back yesterday."

"Come on Arizona, I'm as serious as a heart attack. Let's get him before he gets you. I know for a fact Keith is getting a lot of flak from the sheriff. He's threatened to take over the investigation. The FBI is pretty much out of it for now. Their main objective was the foundation and the money. Think about it. There isn't any other way."

I finished my wine. "How's it you know everything about everything?"

"It's because I'm female. They pay no attention to me at the office. I could stand in the corner anywhere while they are discussing any subject and they wouldn't notice me.

"You know Carter Pane, the other reporter. They know everywhere he is and what he's looking for. Arizona, they will even help him if I'm working on a robbery and he's trying to find a lost dog, his gets the most attention."

I picked up my glass and twirled between two fingers. "Why do you stay there?"

"Two reasons really, I don't make enough money with my art to survive and I enjoy solving the mysteries. Tell me I haven't been a help to you in the murder cases you've solved."

"Of course you have."

I received a beep. When I looked down it was from Keith. *"Where are you? I was by your place, you weren't there."*

Aloud I said, *men.* I answered him. *"Do you need to know everywhere I go? I'm at Liz's."*

"Did you walk?"

"Yes, I walked, Nutmeg is with me."

"Let me know when you're ready to come home. I'll pick you up."

"I'm ready."

Liz walked me downstairs. The three of us waited for my police escort. I wasn't sure I liked his constant attention.

"Are you going to tell him, we want to trap James?"

"I guess, it's the only way we can assure James won't kill me. I'm not going to tell him tonight. Give me a couple of days. I'll have to present it just right. I'll call."

She hugged me when Keith drove up. He rolled down his window and greeted her with a friendly wave.

I opened the door for Nutmeg to jump in the back and then got in the cruiser myself. "Don't you think you are going a little overboard having to know where I am every minute?"

He slowed down and pulled over. "Listen Arizona; don't ever fuss at someone who is trying to protect you. I know James killed Ruth Freedman. You know he killed her. Why do you think he tried to hurt you last week? I guess you think he just wanted to slow you down so the two of you could talk?"

I had been staring straight ahead. I turned to face him. "This could go on forever if we don't figure out how to stop him. I have a great idea."

"And what would that be Officer Summers?"

I glared at him. "Never mind, I'll do it on my own. Liz and I will figure it out." I lied.

"Listen to what you're saying. You and a newspaper reporter have a plan to trap a murderer. Let me guess, you're the bait?"

"Geez Keith, when you say it like that it sounds kind of lame."

"Because it is, I agree we need to do something, but let me think about how to go about it. We won't try anything if I don't think we can protect you."

"We don't have a firm plan. Had you not made me feel like I was twelve, I wouldn't have told you about any of it until we had everything worked out. Liz found out Ruth Freedman ruined James, well, Travis Hall's business on two separate occasions."

He reached over and touched my shoulder. "I'm sorry I hurt your feelings. I'm not sorry it caused you to tell me about what you learned. He might not have meant to kill her. It might have been self-defense but he killed her all the same. We'll work this out together. No rogue operations, promise?"

I didn't answer.

He pulled in front of the apartment and jogged around the car to open my door and to let Nutmeg out. "Don't be mad. I don't think either one of us went about this discussion the right way."

By then I was in a mood. "I didn't know you cared."

He looked me straight in the eye. "You know I do. Call me as soon as you're safe inside."

We walked to the door. Nutmeg walked between us, something she had not done in a very long time.

I went in without saying goodnight. I could be so exasperating, but I couldn't stop myself even when I knew I was wrong.

I took the stairs two at a time, called, said, *I'm inside*, and hung up.

I had a giant character flaw. I hated to be told I was wrong or my ideas wouldn't work.

Which side of the family had the flaw remained a mystery. I did not believe my parents were of sterling quality and character or they would not have given me away destine to live in a foster home until I was eighteen, had it not been for Emma.

Aunt Sandra told me a hundred times I could track down my birth parents. I asked Mom and her answer was the same from the time I first asked to the last time I asked. *It was a closed adoption. You can't see the records*. I'd lived long enough to know there was always a way. I wasn't ready for the truth.

Once I brushed my teeth, washed my face, and finished all my other nightly rituals, I opened the bedroom window, sat in front of it and stared out.

An example of what I considered my biggest flaw came flooding back. Every year Moonstone Lake had a contest. All the kids between ages eight and twelve made rafts. They could be made from paper, cardboard, or anything else we could beg, borrow, or steal. The one that floated the farthest won a huge trophy, a cash prize, and had their picture on the first page of the paper.

Timmy St. John never lost. He had made rafts out of cardboard and duct tape. It scooted to the other side of the lake as if it were power driven, which was not allowed. Only the builder could be on the raft, no sails, motors, or oars.

Three years in a row I came in last. I told Mom and Aunt Sandy I would win the next year because I would make a raft out of paper mache. Mom said it would work if I used mortar instead of glue. Mortar mix wasn't on the approved supply list.

They both told me it would get water logged and sink immediately. I didn't listen. Paper Mache was solid. I'd made masks and volcanoes, and all sorts of projects over the years.

They told me to change my medium if I wanted to win. What did I do? I stayed away from them.

On race day I signed in, got my number, and put my raft in the water to wait for the starting bell. One kid was late; the bottom of my raft began to fall apart, the rest melted while I waited. I didn't get off the launching ramp, one of many cases where I proved how exasperating and stubborn I had always been. I proved to Keith earlier I hadn't changed.

CHAPTER THIRTY-SEVEN

The summer dwellers were back, at least the matriarchs. There were women everywhere. The grocery stores were packed. We were full from morning until night while friends, who hadn't seen each other since the last summer, caught up on a winter's worth of news.

As an owner, I loved the business but the servers were not happy. Two or three women would take up a six seat table. They each needed two chairs. One to sit in and another for the loads of goods they brought in with them. They would chat over two or three cups of coffee. It held up the tables. The fewer customers in a server's area the less tip money they made. Some of the groups would camp out for two or three hours and leave our workers a small tip.

It was Friday and I hadn't had the time to work on the schedule for the next week. I tried to have it up by Wednesday so if someone needed time off I could work around it as I made the timesheet.

At closing time, I walked to the front to talk to Sandy. "I always forget how different the locals are from the squatters."

She shook her head at me. "Are you still calling them squatters? I cringe every time for fear someone will hear you."

I laughed. "How can two groups of people be so different?"

"They don't have much invested here. I can't think of one of them who lives on the north side. Most are over here or somewhere on the lake. Don't get me wrong. They are what keeps The Boardwalk thriving."

"I know. Can you do me a favor? I'm going to sit in my usual spot and finish this schedule before we have anarchy. Can you let everyone out and lock up?"

"Sure. I'm almost done here. I'll check with you before I leave."

"I made myself comfortable, spread out the papers I needed and got started. Nutmeg laid down and spread out on the other bench. She took up the entire space.

Sandy yelled from the doorway. "Okay, money's in the safe, everyone's out of here and I'm going home. Stop by when you get done here."

"Will do."

As I did now and then, I closed my eyes and told myself I needed a life, or at least a hobby.

Nutmeg started her famous grrrrr. She grumbled deep in her throat and she got louder with every sound. I knew I wasn't alone. When I opened my eyes, James walked toward me. He had come from the kitchen.

Nutmeg jumped out of the booth and stopped him in his tracks. She didn't let him get closer than ten feet.

I needed my phone but it was buried under the edge of the pile of papers I used for reference. It would have been impossible to make a call without his knowledge.

"James, I thought everyone went home. Do I need to let you out?"

He pushed Nutmeg with his leg and slid into the seat opposite me. "No, Sandra let me stay to talk to you."

Lie number one, no way Sandra let him stay and didn't mention it to me when she left. I folded my hands in my lap. Maybe if he didn't see my shaking hands he wouldn't pick up on how afraid I was.

Nutmeg moved over to sit at the edge of his side of the booth. No way could he get out without going through the dog.

I knew Nutmeg would lay down her life for me, but I didn't want to test it.

"Could you please call your dog off? This is a friendly visit. I have an idea I want to run by you. Tell her to lie down. Why is she acting like that? She's never growled at me before"

By then Nutmeg had moved closer and now sat an inch away drooling on his pant leg. I didn't say anything to the dog. She had my permission to stay where she was.

James looked down at the dog. "I mean it Arizona.

She is making me nervous."

"Nutmeg come." She looked at me then back to him and then to me again. She didn't move an inch. "Nutmeg. Come." She stood, backed two steps toward me and stood at the ready.

I knew I was in a dangerous situation. I began to sweat. I took one hand out of my lap, pulled a napkin out of the holder on the table and tabbed at my forehead. "What is it you want to see me about that couldn't wait until morning?"

I prayed his idea was not for me to take a swim in Moonstone Lake with weights on my ankles. I took a deep breath and put my papers in a neat pile with my cell phone on top of it. I needed to do my best not to act alarmed.

"I would like us to do more catering, to start a catering company, actually."

If I answered him he would know I was afraid. My voice had a tendency to crack and sometimes not work at all. I willed myself to stay calm. "We do cater."

"Arizona, we don't really. I think we did two weddings last year and one the year before. We took care of one graduation party but they got their cake from Amazin' Glazin'. I mean let's go all out, Moonstone Lake Café' and Catering. I'll find the gigs, make the food, get my own servers, and use your equipment. You can have half of the gross receipts."

I didn't answer right away. If I said no, would he kill me? How he got inside the café bothered me more than anything. Aunt Sandy locked up hundreds of times. He was not there by accident. I put my other hands back in my lap so they didn't shake. "It might be a good idea had we not just spent thousands of dollars on a new buffet bar, paint, flooring, and new upholstering for the booths. It doesn't go in until the first week of June. It's a lot of money.

"I'll tell you what, put everything you have on paper and as soon as we get used to the new buffet we can take a hard look at it. I don't want to take on too much at once."

He adjusted in the booth and when he did, he was somehow closer to me.

Nutmeg jumped up from where she sat and went back to sit by his leg.

James didn't say anything about her but he gave her a look. "I owned a catering company once back east. It was a real money maker until we had a stroke of bad luck."

"What happened?"

"It's a story for another day. I interrupted your work as it is."

My phone rang. It was Keith. *Oh hi, Chief.*

He: *I know you don't like it, but I wanted to know if you made it home safe and sound.*

Me: *I'm sorry. I thought I'd be done with the schedule. What time does it start?*

Keith: *You're not alright are you?*

Me: *James and I are in the main dining room talking about starting a catering company. He'll understand. He was just leaving.*

Keith: *I'm on my way.*

Me: *We'll make it. I look respectable enough to go, that'll save time. Even if we are late the previews take at least ten minutes.*

James slid out of the booth but instead of going toward the door, he took a step toward me. Nutmeg grabbed his pant leg.

"Nutmeg, Let go of James. I can't imagine why she is acting like that, can you?"

"I can't think of anything unless I have something on my hands or clothes she doesn't like."

Nutmeg backed off. She was not a happy dog.

CHAPTER THIRTY-EIGHT

I heard Keith skid up to the back door. I opened it and he stepped in. I'm not a crier, but I couldn't help it. He opened his arms and I melted into them. My entire body trembled. Once I was under control he let go. "Tell me what happened."

I looked around the kitchen and whispered to him. "Not here."

His eyes followed the path mine had taken a second earlier. "Why not here?"

"I think he left..."

He took hold of my upper arms. "What do you mean you *think* he left?"

"I didn't let him in and I didn't let him out. For all I know, he's still in here."

"Stay here while I make sure he's gone." He took my hand and led me into the supply closet. Don't move until I come back to get you. Where was

Nutmeg during all of this? I'm surprised she didn't tear him apart."

I shrugged my shoulders. "I held her back. I treated him as I though I didn't know we suspected him of anything."

"If he comes back, let her go. She can hold her own."

It could have been five minutes; it could have been a half-an-hour. I sat on the floor, bent my knees, put my forearms on them and laid my head on my arms. Nutmeg stood guard by the door. Why did James feel the need to let me know he could come and go as he pleased? If he was out to scare me, he did a bang up job.

Keith came back with his gun holstered. He reached down to take both of my hands and help me up.

The motion detector flashed. It indicated someone was on the move inside the building. He drew his gun again. "Stay here. I'll check it out and be right back."

As soon as he rounded the corner I followed.

When I caught up with him he and Sandra were near the pass through door. He turned to look at me. "I told you to stay put. Do you ever listen?"

I didn't bother to answer. Instead I gave Sandy a brief synopsis of what happened, "It's not reassuring he can come and go as he wants."

Nutmeg barked.

Aunt Sandy put her hands on her hips. "I want you to know I let him out like everyone else and I locked the door behind him. I remember because he went back to get a book he left in the kitchen. I had to stand by the backdoor and wait for him."

Nutmeg ran toward the kitchen. We all followed. She pawed under the back door until I turned off the alarm and Keith opened it. The dog stayed where she was and sniffed the door jam. She looked at me and barked.

I got on my knees and so did the other two. There was a wad of some sort of putty between the door jam and the bottom of the door.

"Can one of you get me a small plastic bag so I can take a sample of this back to the lab?"

Aunt Sandy went to get it. She held it open and Keith picked up a piece of it with his pocketknife. When he finished, he cleaned the rest of it off so the door would again make contact with the frame.

"I'd like it if you'd set the alarms. We'll go out the back and I'll walk you ladies home.

"Thanks for rescuing me. Well, maybe it wasn't a rescue, but Nutmeg changed her mind about him and decided he was not a friend. I find that unsettling."

Aunt Sandy said, "I'm going home. You kids don't stay up too late. My cats and I are going to get cozy with a good book and a glass of wine."

"Do you have wine in your apartment?" Keith asked.

My mind went through quick analysis of my place, dishes in the sink. My clothes on the chairs, every pair of shoes I owned lying about, and the bathrooms and both bedrooms trashed. "We'll have to have wine another night. I'm exhausted from my encounter with James. I'd like a hot bath and to go to bed so I can calm down. Thanks again for the rescue. Liz and I haven't come up with a plan to catch him.

I didn't realize until tonight how big he is, and intimidating."

He put his hand under my chin and lifted it so I looked him in the eyes. "I beg you not to do this on your own. I'd hate to see anything happen to you." He kissed me lightly on the lips and left

CHAPTER THIRTY-NINE

We had a wild Memorial weekend at Moonstone Lake. The shops, sidewalks, outdoor cafés, and the arcade all overflowed with people as well as an extra hundred boats on the lake.

Every time I checked on James he was the sweet, calm, unflappable guy I knew before he tried to hurt me on the trail. I still hadn't figured out a good reason why he did it. Keith told me to go on as though nothing had happened so long as James did the same.

It was easier said than done to try to dismiss him and his antics of the week before. Every time I passed him I held my breath and prayed nothing would happen. He didn't mention the catering company again. Maybe he was on a fact finding visit when he came in after hours.

I thought if ignoring a possible murderer's bad behavior was Keith's idea of how to trip him up, it was stupid and dangerous.

We were all exhausted on June first but it didn't matter. We served brunch and cleaned up quickly. A crew from the kitchen equipment company came in as did the painting crew. The flooring people would put down the floor under the new system.

Sandy, Mom, Lewis, James, and the entire serving crew, including the line cooks showed up to help. We had to reopen on Tuesday morning.

Keith stopped by twice. The first time he asked to speak to me alone. "The substance under the door was corn starch putty. Ever hear of it?"

"Sure, its corn starch and liquid dish soap. Kids can play with it for hours then it gets hard and breaks into small pieces that look like wood."

"How do you know that?"

"As a child, my mom and I would make it in the morning. Sometimes it would last all day. Once in a while she put food coloring in it."

"Any around now? It's the substance that kept the door from latching the other night so James could come and go."

"Clever idea, you would have to make it close to the time you want to use it. It's air that makes the consistency change. I need to get back in there. They are liable to put something in backward."

The second time he came he brought tacos from Bueno Taco on the Boardwalk. The entire group took a break. Leon, a line cook, got plastic cups from the supply closet and we all sat on the floor and ate.

I leaned over to Keith. "This is really nice of you."

"You're welcome."

Someone brought Mom a stool from the kitchen.

I glanced around the room. Mom had three of the younger servers mesmerized with a story. Sandy and Lewis were talking about a book he read. Everyone looked happy. When I glanced in James direction, He sat alone at the edge of the room. I caught him looking at me. He quickly turned his head.

Nutmeg chewed on a rawhide bone I kept in the drawer up front for her.

Keith asked, "Did you have enough to eat?"

"Looks like they all did. Thanks again. I'd better crack the whip or we won't be ready to open Tuesday morning."

"How can you do this for two and a half days and then go to work?

I grinned at him. "I'd like to say I'm super woman, but I am off Tuesday. So are Sandy, Lewis and James. The line cooks and serving staff can handle it. It's a slow day. It's why I picked it."

"Okay, I have to go. Crime doesn't take a day off. Petty offenses have picked up since Memorial Day."

"The city folk are here."

Later in the evening I was making fresh coffee in the kitchen when Liz called. "It's going well. I think we will make our deadline...really? Travis Hall had a third catering company. Where was it? ...Oh, I see...he's here with the rest of us."

Nutmeg growled. I turned and there stood James. "Who's Travis Hall?" he asked.

I know I turned white because I had the sensation I would pass out as the blood left my head."

Nutmeg sensed it. She pushed between me and James and moved him back. When I could focus again, I saw his face. His big blue eyes were slits of anger. His fists were clenched. He started to take a step toward me but Nutmeg grabbed his leg.

He picked up a skillet and held it in the air. "Call her off Arizona. I swear I'll kill her. She bit me once, I don't intend for her to do it again."

"Why did you hurt me on the path?"

He lowered the pan and Nutmeg took a step back toward me. "Because I knew you would find the glove as soon as I walked out the door. And I was correct. I put a pencil mark on the bag so I could tell if anyone touched it. You just couldn't leave well enough alone."

"After all I have learned about Ruth Freedman and the horrible things she did to you, you have a solid defense. Give yourself up. Don't make it worse. You're not a killer."

"No Arizona, I'm not, but a person can only take so much. She ruined my business and made it impossible for me to start over. The look on her face, when she saw me in the kitchen the day they came to the buffet, was one of triumph. There we were, together in the same place. She couldn't wait to tell me she would ruin me again. And you're wrong about me being innocent. They believe I poisoned her but I didn't. They'll say it was premeditated."

I took a deep breath to try and relax a bit. "Then, who did?"

"I'm not convinced anyone did. It was one of the problems with catering for her. She had at least a dozen allergies and didn't pay attention to what she ate. She picked something up, ate it and then asked what was in it. Stupid. Stupid. Hateful woman."

"So what happened between you two?"

"I was upset and tired of waiting for the other shoe to fall. I went for a walk and ended up on the dock.

"She was at the top of the hill having an argument with somebody. She came down the hill stumbling like a drunk. The minute she saw me, she started telling me how she would ruin me. She called me Ptomaine Travis.

"I lost my temper and pushed her in the water. She didn't move or even try to move. I panicked and took one of the boats from the dock and dragged her out to a different part of the lake."

I tried to back away from him. "James. It sounds as if she died from something else."

"Arizona it doesn't matter at this point. Even if she died of something I didn't do, after I kill you it won't matter at all."

Nutmeg lunged for him. Her weight knocked him into a chair. The chair tipped over and he landed on his front side, his face got the brunt of it. He was stunned.

I picked up the heavy pan and held it like a baseball bat. Before I could call 911, Keith came through the front door, gun drawn. Randy Malone came in from the kitchen.

"How did you know to come?"

"Liz heard him ask you who Travis Hall was. She called it in. We've heard the entire conversation. We have him dead to rights."

James began to stand. Randy took one of his arms and then the other and handcuffed him. I heard, *you have* the right to *remain silent* as they left.

The Moonstone Lake Reflection ran a feature article about the case and how the police got there man. Liz couldn't help but talk about my part and my remarkable dog.

FORTY

The authorities housed James in the Moonstone Lake jail until they were able to transfer him to the county facility. Keith wanted me to press charges for the assault. I couldn't do it. I had no trouble seeing why he hated Ruth Freedman.

The trial lasted three weeks. Several people from Boston and New York corroborated his story about how she destroyed his business twice.

The samples of her blood and tissue had come back from the state laboratory. No one there could identify the substance in her body as a poison.

Dillon and Roger Freedman took the stand and told about her many food allergies and how she indiscriminately tasted foods without regard to her own safety.

The coroner said she had no water in her lungs and most likely died of a heart attack before she hit the water.

James couldn't get off scot free because he purposely held her in the water with the intent of killing her if she hadn't already passed. He was charged with involuntary manslaughter, abusing a corpse and hindering a police investigation.

The tenth time Keith told me James wanted to see me; I drove to the county seat. I got there the day before they were to move him to the prison in Potosí.

I'd never been to the county jail and hoped never to go again. Keith wanted to escort me but I declined.

A guard met me at the front gate. "Driver's license please."

I handed it to him. "I'm here to see…"

Without looking up he interrupted me. "I know who you are here to see. Drive straight down this lane until you reach the parking lot. Park in the first row marked, visitor. Don't take anything inside the building with you."

I held my hand out to retrieve my ID.

He tapped it on the clipboard he held. "You'll be able to pick it up on your way out."

He sneered when I told him to, "Have a nice day."

When I reached the front door, I was buzzed in by an armed guard. "Follow me." Was all he said.

I followed, silently.

We went through an electric barred door. It opened with a loud clang and closed behind us so quickly, I jumped.

James was housed in the third visitor's room on my left. They buzzed me in through a solid wooden door with a barred window.

He sat in a chair pushed up to a scarred wooden

table in the middle of the room. An armed guard stood behind him with his arms crossed against his chest and a blank look on his face.

James stood, I assumed to hug me. The officer stepped up. "No touching allowed."

I sat in the only other chair in the room, on the other side of the table.

He had aged five years, had two day stubble, the brightness had left his eyes. I could only describe him as defeated.

I waited a long minute, but he didn't speak. I guessed it was up to me. "You wanted to see me, James?"

He looked me in the eyes. "I wanted to apologize before I leave here. Saying I'm sorry will in no way make up for my hurting you, yet I had to tell you in person how sorry and embarrassed I am for my actions."

I had no idea what to say.

He went on. "When I saw the name on the catering slip for the wedding, I panicked."

"I understand that but had you come to me and told me what she did to you; I could have kept the two of you apart."

"Arizona, I have gone over what I did hundreds of times in my mind. What I should have done and what I did are so far apart. I saw Ruth at the top of the hill and went to beg her not to ruin my life again. She laughed. I could tell she didn't feel well, but I didn't move a hand to help her.

"She stumbled down the hill to the dock and fell into the water. I untied one of the Jon boats and went to help her out of the water.

"There she was, floating face down. She didn't move a muscle. I don't know what came over me. I dragged her alongside the boat and wedged her under the end of the dock so she would stay put.

"It was like I had left my body and watched myself with no control over my actions. All I could hear was her despicable laugh and chiding voice as she threatened to ruin me, for the third time.

"After that night, things snowballed. I have no excuse for myself. I'll have five years in prison to search my soul. When I found out she had no water in her lungs and there was nothing I could have done to help her, I realized I was as wicked as she was. I wanted to explain what I did. You and the people at the restaurant have been like family and I ruined it all because of my lack of trust."

Tears streamed down his face, he wiped them away with the back of his hand. I didn't quite know what to say. "James, we all make mistakes. For my part, I forgive you. When you get out of jail, I will give you a reference. It's all I can do. I would never be able to trust you again. Best of luck to you. I hope your life settles down."

He said nothing else. He stood and walked to the guard. They left by way of a door on the other side of the room.

THE END

About the Author

Susan Keene, author of the popular Kate Nash Mystery series, lives in the Ozarks and writes full time.

She loves to cook, hang out with her grandchildren, and spend time with her numerous dogs.

Susan's new series, The Arizona Summers Mysteries are true cozies. They include a restaurant, her mother, who doesn't want to let go of the business, although she retired years earlier and her Aunt and best friend Sandy.

Nutmeg helps her solve crimes and keeps her out of harm's way. The dog is able to know what is going to happen just before it does. Some have begun to call her psychic.

Each book includes recipes for some of the dishes that were used somewhere in each adventure.

RECIPES

ASPARAGUS STUFFED PORTABELLA MUSHROOMS
The dish Arizona took to Roger Freedmen's open house.
INGREDIENTS:
4 large portabella mushrooms
1 tablespoon virgin olive oil
2 teaspoons virgin olive oil
1 ½ cups fresh asparagus, cut (five or six spears)
1/3 cup sweet onion, chopped
2 fresh garlic cloves, minced
1 large tomato
salt and pepper to taste
1 cup panko bread crumbs
¼ cup of parmesan or romano grated cheese
Parsley flakes

DIRECTIONS: PREP TIME 35 minutes
    1. Preheat oven to 400 degrees
    2. Cut stems and chop into small pieces, set aside
    3. Clean gills from mushrooms with a spoon, rinse them in cold water and pat dry with a towel
    4. Brush the two tablespoons of olive oil on the back of the mushrooms.
    5. Place oiled side down on a baking sheet
    6. Heat one of the teaspoons of oil in a non-stick skillet over medium heat.
    7. Add asparagus, onions, garlic, and chopped mushroom stems. Cook 5-6 minutes until vegetables are tender yet crisp. Stir occasionally
    8. Remove from heat and stir in tomatoes, salt and pepper and spoon mixture into mushrooms.
    9. Combine bread crumbs and cheese and sprinkle over mushrooms.
    10.   Mix the parley and the rest of the olive oil over bread crumbs.

11.   Bake 10-12 minutes and the bread crumbs are golden brown.

CHICKEN AND THREE CHEESE CASSEROLE *One of the new dishes for the buffet*
INGREDIENTS:
4 cups cooked chicken diced (I boil mine and use breasts)
2 tablespoons butter
One small chopped sweet onion
¾ cup green pepper
1 can Cream of Chicken soup
1 can sliced mushrooms, drained.
½ tablespoon dried basil
1 package (8 oz) of egg noodles, cooked and drained
2 cups grated cheddar cheese
2 cups cottage cheese
½ cup grated parmesan cheese
DIRECTIONS:
Sauté onion and peppers in the butter until tender.
Remove from heat and add soup, mushrooms, and basil, set aside.
Mix together noodles, chicken, cheddar cheese, cottage cheese and parmesan cheese.
Pour soup mixture over noodles and combine. Pour into greased 9x13 inch baking dish.
Bake 350 degrees for 50 minutes

BONUS! TWO INGREDIENT RECIPES

EASY CAKE
One 15 ½ oz can of real pumpkin, one spice cake mix. Add the pumpkin and the cake mix together and mix on high until they are cake batter consistency. Add nothing else. Bake using directions on box of cake mix.

LEMON CAKE BARS
One can lemon pie filling and one box of angel food cake mix.
Mix with electric mixer until thoroughly
Bake according to directions on cake box.
You might want to sprinkle the top with powdered sugar.